Sparrow's Gun

Before setting off in pursuit of the men who murdered his father, Will Sparrow learns how to handle a gun. Rufus Joad teaches him, but from then on, the old ranch-hand can only stand by and watch.

Many miles from his home, Will gets himself a job as a stable boy while he plans his reprisal on Oliver Patch and Tel Judkins. But then Laurel Wale happens along, and Will discovers his intentions aren't quite as clear-cut as he thought. To further complicate matters, Will's mother has settled down nearby with one of the territory's most important citizens. She wants nothing more than peace and to make amends for a previous family indiscretion, but nothing is going to deter Will from his fateful objective. With his loyal friend Rufus watching his back, Will prepares to confront the men he's travelled so far to kill.

Sparrow's Gun

Abe Dancer

A Black Horse Western

ROBERT HALE · LONDON

© Abe Dancer 2014
First published in Great Britain 2014

ISBN 978-0-7198-1265-1

Robert Hale Limited
Clerkenwell House
Clerkenwell Green
London EC1R 0HT

www.halebooks.com

Typeset by
Derek Doyle & Associates, Shaw Heath
Printed and bound in Great Britain by
CPI Antony Rowe, Chippenham and Eastbourne

1

Rufus Joad's holster and cartridge belt were of the same tan leather. The back of the holster carried the small brandmark, CJ. The gun was a single-action .36 Navy Colt revolver that was the favourite of soldiers and civilians alike; one of the finest pistols ever made. But Joad's wasn't a regular model. His was blue steel, with the darkness not in any enamel, but in the metal itself. The grip was walnut, and two small ivory discs were set into it, one on each side.

Will Sparrow held it up to aiming level, feeling the balance in his hand. It was clean and polished and oiled. When he flicked the empty cylinder, it spun swiftly and noiselessly.

'Just show me how to use it, Rufus. An' I don't mean for scaring off a mangy coyote,' he said, grinding his teeth, breathing deep against the sup-pressed wrath.

'I'll show you, Will. But remember, although it's a fine gun, it's *you* who's going to make the killing. Don't ever remove yourself from that thought. Not before or after.'

Will took another look at the rig, then buckled it around his waist, fixed the tie-down laces. 'I'll remember, Rufus,' he said. 'I wouldn't have it any other way. And I'll be paying you like for any other tool.'

'That's up to you,' Joad said, and immediately started on his lesson. 'That's it. Set the holster, so you're not stretching or reaching. Have it so the grip's just above your wrist. That way you can take the gun as your hand's coming up. There's room to clear your holster without having to lift the gun too high.'

Joad watched while Will adjusted the holster and belt until it was set comfortable, then he continued. 'Some men have their own tricks . . . stuff to look out for. If there's one who likes a shoulder holster, there's another who packs his gun in his pants belt. There's some who carry two guns, but that's usually for exhibition and a waste of weight. One's enough, if you know how to use it. I once saw a feller in Durango who had a tight holster with an open end. It was fastened on a little swivel to the belt. He didn't have to pull the gun, just swing up the barrel and blaze away. That was the idea, anyway.'

6

'Why? What happened to him?'

'One night he was standing out back of some saloon taking a piss, and got a big ol' Green River knife wedged between his shoulder blades. I'm telling you all this, Will, to try and keep you alive.'

'Yeah, I know. So what about aiming? For what I've got in mind, hitting the target's real important.'

'Hold it so the barrel's right in line with your fingers held out straight. If you don't have time, don't waste any by bringing it up high. It should all come together in one smooth move. Slip back the hammer as you bring the gun up and squeeze the trigger straight off when you've got the level. Make it quick an' easy, like pointing a finger ... like you're showing 'em what you're about to do.'

'Yeah. I want to see their faces when that dawns on them.'

'But there's always going to be someone outside of the generality,' Joad offered. 'Watch their eyes, their mouth. If you want *them* dead, and *you* to live, you'll walk away. Meantime, you practise, Will. That's the means.'

The man from the Wolf Run ranch gave Will a long, searching look, then he turned and walked away.

2

Wanting a better look at the stranger who'd ridden towards the livery, the sheriff of Magdalena stepped from his office. He sniffed, spat a thin ribbon of tobacco juice on to the boardwalk.

'Another goddamn gunslinger,' he muttered.

'Is that you sayin' or just guessin'?' Cooter Lennon asked.

As he turned to his deputy, Ambrose Wale didn't take his eyes off the stranger. 'I ain't seen a dodger, if that's what you mean, Cooter. Best you go check him out, though. Let him see your badge.'

'Yeah, I thought you'd be sayin' that. Goin' to see if strangers in town are either gunnies or cowpokes is gettin' to be a habit,' the deputy sighed.

'Just do it,' Wale snapped, then watched as Cooter stepped down into the street, strolling casually to the town livery. In Wale's opinion, Cooter Lennon was a good young man, tough and honest, if not a tad reckless at times. But Juno Hemsby, Wale's second deputy, was an older and wiser bird, and Wale wished he were there, instead of out at the Rochester Ranch.

The stranger was talking to the hostler about the care of his fine buckskin mare. He was in his mid-twenties, standing around six foot, wearing travel-stained denims and prick spurs around his boots. Under the sweat-stained range hat, his hair was corn-coloured. His side arm was a single-action Navy Colt .36, carried in a tie-down holster. After a short conversation, he handed over some money, turned purposefully and continued up the street.

From outside of the livery doors where he'd been waiting and watching, Cooter cursed and hitched his gunbelt higher around his waist. Then he cursed again and strode off in the man's footsteps. 'Hang on, feller,' he called out. 'I'd like a word . . . if you don't mind.'

The man stopped, turned slowly and eyed the deputy. 'An' if I do?' he said with a tight, not unfriendly smile.

Cooter halted not too close, not too far from him. 'That ain't likely, this bein' your first day in town an' all,' he said. 'Please state your name an' business.'

The stranger nodded. 'William Sparrow. But with respect, my business is my business,' he replied softly with a glance at Cooter's metal star of office.

9

'It's all there if you think about it.'

'Thinkin' don't figure for deputies. I'm carryin' out the sheriff's orders.'

Sparrow stared back at Cooter with cold, grey eyes. 'I understand that, officer. Would there be anything else?'

Cooter flushed, rubbed the heel of his hand against his hip. 'How long you figure on stayin' in town?'

Sparrow looked past the deputy to the sheriff's office. 'I don't know. It depends,' he said pensively, seeing the heavy figure of Ambrose Wale staring his way.

Cooter half closed his eyes as if another thought came to mind. 'Are you here lookin' for someone? Is *that* your business?'

'If I am, you'll get to hear of it. I promise.' For a moment, Sparrow held Cooter with another intimidating look, then he turned and walked on to the Spanish Peaks Hotel.

Almost breaking into a run, Cooter caught up with Sparrow, reaching out, grasping him by the elbow. It was only a brief touch, but Cooter felt the immediate tremor of fear.

Sparrow spun around, took two quick paces back. 'That's a real stupid thing to do, Deputy. Don't ever do it again,' he said abruptly. Then he turned his back, before Cooter could continue his questioning.

10

Two men ran across the street to find out what was going on, to see if the deputy needed any help. 'Proddy bastard,' Cooter growled, brushing off their inquiries, as well as his useless confrontation.

'Have you got a single room?' Will Sparrow asked of the hotel desk clerk.

'Yep.' The clerk pushed the ledger towards him. 'Sign here for the key.' He watched Will write his name, then he handed him a tagged key. 'Room Four.'

'I've not seen scrub water for a while. Can I get a bath?'

'Yep. Right on down the hall. I'll get some soap an' hot water sent up.'

Will nodded his thanks. 'Include a bottle of whiskey . . . one with a label,' he said, and without a look back, walked on up the stairs to his room.

An hour later he was suitably liquored, bathed and shaved and feeling refreshed. The aches of many weeks in the saddle were still in his bones, but a good sleep would fix that, he told himself. He locked the door and jammed the back of a rocking chair under the knob. After carefully placing the bottle of whiskey on the floor beside him, he stretched out on the bed. Within five minutes he was asleep, his Colt tucked under the end of the pillow.

*

Cooter Lennon was back in the sheriff's office, making his excuses. 'His name's Sparrow. William Sparrow,' he said. 'He's from out o' town, an' got some sort o' business at Spanish Peaks.'

'Yeah, bed an' breakfast business. Goddamnit it, Cooter, I saw most o' what happened,' Wale rasped. 'He made as if you were goose egg. You're wearin' a badge, for Chris' sakes.'

'You think that'll stop a bullet?' Did you see that piece o' his from where you were standin'?'

'Don't get sassy, kid. He saw me too. I'm thinkin' it's why he didn't slap you down when you laid a hand on him.'

'I got his name, didn't I?'

The sheriff glared up at Cooter from behind his scarred desk. 'If he's goin' to use that hogleg to kill somebody, his name ain't likely real cheese, is it?' Nor would it be if he was on a goddamn dodger.'

As if in agreement, Cooter shook his head. 'I saw somethin' in his eyes, though. Except that's another thing you couldn't see from here.'

'I told you already, Cooter, cut the lip. Besides, the only eyes you've been takin' notice of lately is them doey peepers o' young Elodie Wesker,' he added a little more kindly.

Cooter grinned sheepishly. 'OK, don't start that again. It's bad enough havin' to put up with Juno's chaff.'

'Then why the hell don't you marry her?'

12

Cooter walked over to the window, looked out at the folk milling around in doorways and at street corners. 'Maybe I will,' he said. 'An' maybe real soon.'

Wale grinned. 'Come on. We'll do the rounds, then have some grub,' he suggested.

The two lawmen stepped on to the boardwalk. Cooter headed east and Wale turned west.

The sheriff carried the weightiness of middle age. He was turning grey at the temples and his tanned face showed lines. He wore a pistol, but when taking a turn of the town he also carried a big revolving shotgun in the crook of his arm.

Out at the corral sheds, Cooter took a long look around before starting back. He was approaching the jailhouse, when he saw Juno Hemsby riding in from the west. He grinned and lifted a hand in greeting, waiting for him to rein in at the hitchrail.

Hemsby was a tall man and slim, his mustachios and long hair fittingly rope-coloured. 'How's Romeo Lennon makin' out?' he asked agreeably.

'He's doin' fine. What took you so long, Juno?'

'I didn't know that Farley Rochester had such a good-lookin' niece, Cooter. I could've spent all day out there just a-lookin'.' Hemsby sat his horse easily, a no-nonsense Colt Dragoon strapped to his thigh. 'Yessir, County's money well spent, if you ask me.'

'I'd find some other way of explainin' that to Wale if I were you.'

Hemsby's shoulders sagged. 'Grumpy, eh?'

Cooter nodded. 'Yeah. You know how he is when there's another stranger in town.'

'Who is it this time . . . the stranger? Anythin' on him?'

'Name's William Sparrow. That's all he wanted to give me.'

Hemsby swung down from the saddle and tied in the reins. 'Never heard of him. What's he like?'

'I don't know. We didn't exactly hit it off. He's no hay-shaker, that's for sure. He's got hair like it, though.'

'That's not quite enough to peg him as trouble, Cooter.' Hemsby stepped up to the jailhouse door. 'Anythin' else happen while I was away?'

'Nope,' Cooter said as he followed him into the office. 'How'd you get on?' he asked.

'Ah, I'm too old for her, Cooter. She'd be the death o' me.'

'I meant the fight.'

'Oh, that. Turns out someone called Gall killed someone called Chebber. It was a fair fight, or so the other hands reckon.'

'What were they fightin' over? Rochester's niece?'

Hemsby gave Cooter an amused, inquiring look. 'Wale make you some sort of investigator, did he, while I was away?'

Cooter shuffled his feet and grinned. 'He said I was to learn, find out, take an interest.'

14

'Good. He's right. Where is he, by the way?'

'Still walkin' the town, I guess. He should've been back by now.'

3

Will Sparrow opened his eyes when he heard the knock. He reached under the pillow and gripped his Colt, then rolled off the bed and walked over to the door.

'Who's there?' he called.

'Ambrose Wale. Open up.'

Will moved the chair away with his foot, opened the door to the grim set of the sheriff. 'What's going on?' he asked.

'A little earlier, one o' my deputies asked you your business. He didn't get an answer,' Wale said calmly.

'That's right. There's no law against it, is there?'

Wale's eyes narrowed. 'No, not always. But he was doin' what he was told. So if you give any o' my men disrespect when you're asked a civil question again, I might not take it so lightly. You understand?'

Will moved a shoulder in a slight shrug. 'Yes,

16

Sheriff. Is there anything else?'

'You really ain't made a great start, mister, drawin' my attention an' all. So walk easy,' Wale snapped, holding Will's cold stare.

'Like I told your deputy, I just want to mind my own business, Sheriff. That's all.'

'Well, let's hope it don't become mine. Time being, you can put that Colt away an' wedge the chair back against the door. Goodnight.'

Will stood in the doorway until Wale was out of sight. Then he slammed the door shut and cursed at being capably bettered. A minute later he buttoned up his shirt and dragged on his boots. He strapped on his gunbelt, picked up his hat and left the room.

It was well into full dark as he walked to the Rugosa Saloon. He pushed at the batwings and went in, quickly stepping to one side from innate instinct. The smoke was hanging low and thick and there were quite a few customers scattered about the long room. He made his way to the bar, avoiding some men grouped around a discordant piano.

'I'll have a beer,' he said.

'Your folks never learn the word "*please*"?' the barkeep asked in a manner that wasn't meant to be taken too lightly.

There were loud, crude noises from drinkers standing nearby who had obviously been waiting for something to amuse them. 'Please, mister. Mama says I'm to have a fruit sarsaparilla,' one of them muttered in a squeaky voice.

Will took a deep breath. 'Glad to give you all a laugh, but my pa taught me there's only certain things in life to say please for. What *you* provide's certainly not one of 'em, you ugly son-of-a-bitch,' he said. 'Meantime, I'll have that beer.'

'You're either brave or stupid, sonny. I'm favourin' stupid,' the barkeep scowled.

Will's left arm shot forward. His hand grabbed the barkeep's choker and dragged him half over the wet, slippy bar top. Then the thumb of his right hand jabbed into the man's face, hard up against the nose bone. 'An' my ma sucked lamp oil from a crock,' he said in low voice. 'Now pour me my beer . . . *please.*'

The room had become almost silent. The barkeep rubbed his nose, but without another word poured Will his beer.

As if nothing had happened, Will slipped his change into his pocket and took his beer over to a far table. He sat with his back to the wall, watching the doors.

Fifteen minutes passed before a bunch of cowhands entered. Calling for drinks as they pushed their way to the bar, one of them shouted at the piano player. 'Hey, Tunes, give us somethin' for kickin' heels.'

Will's eyes flicked over them one by one before

18

dismissing them as of little or no interest. Another five minutes ticked by, then a man dressed in an expensive town suit walked up to Will's table.

'Mind if I sit?' he asked.

'There's other places. Besides, I'm not feeling too sociable at the moment.'

'Yeah, I apologize for that. My name's Addison Rugosa and for my sins, I'm the proprietor.'

'Well, your bar dog's got a big mouth,' Will said without looking up. 'He's lucky it's still full of teeth.'

'It's a saloon, for Chris'sakes, not Sunday School.' Rugosa smiled genially. 'These cowboys usually take all that in their stride. Don't let our Cato get under your skin.'

Will glanced up. 'He doesn't get under my skin, and I'm not a cowboy,' he said.

'Are you here looking for work?'

'No.'

Rugosa seemed to irritate slightly at Will's cool distance. 'I could use a good man right now. Not a cowboy, you understand. Are you interested?'

'Like I said, I'm not looking for work.'

The saloonist's eyes hardened. He started to move away but stopped. 'What's your name?'

'Will Sparrow.'

'Well, Will Sparrow, the offer's there. If you do start looking . . .' he said, letting his words drift off, moving away through the noisy blend of customers.

'I'll bear it in mind,' Will replied quietly. He saw

19

Cato huggermugger with a few of the ranch-hands, looking his way and nodding. Eventually, two men pushed their way over to him. One, a bull-necked giant, stood close, grinning.

'You pretty fancy at pokin' faces,' he snorted.

Will didn't answer, just stared back.

'Cato is a friend, an' we don't take kindly to him gettin' so treated,' the second man warned. He spat at Will's feet, hitting the toe of his boot. He was a small, dark, wiry man; looked as though he was a sharp mover.

'So I guess we'll see how you like it,' the big man said.

They took a step closer, but stopped for a moment when Will held up his left hand.

The giant thought for another moment, then snorted again. The small man sniggered and together they moved in.

Will's right hand hardly appeared to move. But suddenly there it was, resting on the table holding the .36 Colt, aimed straight at the big man's gut.

'It'll be you first,' he said, matter-of-factly. 'Think carefully.'

The cowboy swallowed hard, paled and broke into a sweat.

Will raised the barrel of the Colt, looked from one man to the other. 'I've just been told you boys . . . like funning around. Well, sometimes I don't think it's such a good idea. So back off to where you just come from.' He rose to his feet as they retreated. 'Hey, feller. You've got some cleaning to do,' he called out to the small man, putting his foot on the seat of a nearby chair. 'Ask your friend Cato for a cloth.'

The man shook his head. 'Not me, boy. I don't clean nobody's boots.'

'OK,' Will said and stepped swiftly forward. With his left hand he gave a short punch low into the man's stomach. 'That's just *me* funning,' he said as the man crumpled, grunting, to the sawdusted puncheons.

'Hell, you shouldn't have done that, kid. He's mean an' irritable . . . carries a grudge. We don't call him Ratsnake for nothin',' the big man growled.

'What the hell is it with you people?' Will rasped.

The two men locked menacing stares for a moment, then the big man helped the suffering cowhand outside.

Will gave them ten minutes, then he too walked from the saloon. He didn't look around him, just felt all eyes on his back as he went.

4

Ambrose Wale grumbled an oath when one of the drinkers from the Rugosa Saloon finished telling him about the incident that had just happened.

'An' you're sure it was Rochester hands who started it?'

'Certain, Sheriff,' the pinched-featured owner of Baxter's Mercantile replied. 'The boys were just out for a little fun . . . probably weren't meaning to hurt anyone.'

Wale gave his doubtful stare. 'It's *their* kind o' fun that gets someone killed. Anyway, thanks for lettin' me know, Mose.'

Baxter nodded, then started for the door but stopped when Wale called out.

'Who was it that this feller Sparrow floored?'

'Polk Chatham. The one they call Ratsnake.'

'Good. I mean, yeah, it would be. Thanks again, Mose.' Wale turned to Juno Hemsby. 'This Will

22

Sparrow's stirrin' up the dust, Juno,' he said. 'I'll go look for him, have a word in his shell-like. You go find Chatham. Tell him I want no more trouble.'

Wale watched Hemsby leave, then he went to the gun rack and lifted his shotgun. He loaded up the cylinder's big shot chambers, took time to think for a few moments, before leaving the jailhouse.

He found Will Sparrow standing calm and thoughtful, inside the livery barn. 'I got a report there was trouble in the saloon. I heard it was between you an' three or four Rochester cowboys,' he stated.

'You heard quick, even for a small town. But there was only two of them,' Will corrected.

'Was it right you pulled your gun?'

'Yeah. Only for a moment, though.'

Wale nodded grimly. 'Them cowboys usually carry cheap irons to look scary. I'm guessin' that ain't the same in your case, Sparrow. I'll overlook it this time, seein' as there was more'n one of 'em.'

'I'll try an' not let it happen again.' Will, who appeared to be not too concerned, turned his attention to a gentle tugging of an ear.

'Polk Chatham's got a nasty streak to him,' Wale continued. 'If he does come lookin' to make more of it, back down. I reckon you're capable o' that.'

'Wouldn't be easy.'

'So it's difficult.' Wale sighed. 'Look, Sparrow, for a moment, just indulge me. Pretend you ain't so goddamn hard-nosed. That trouble you had tonight was with the Rochester crew. Now, Rochester's a mighty big augur in these parts . . . be real huffy if anythin' bad happened to one of his boys. There'd be reprisals.'

'Has it crossed your mind, Sheriff, that I'm just not interested in this Rochester man's crew, or any other crew for that matter? So if *you* don't want real trouble, *you* warn them off. I'm not aimin' to go anywhere just yet, certainly with my tail between my legs. That's all I'm saying.'

Wale took an uncertain breath. 'Yeah, I guess that'll have to do. Travel hopefully, eh? Just for the sake of askin', if you won't tell me what you're here for, perhaps you'll tell me when you're going?'

'Like I told your deputy; when my business is done. When it *is*, you'll be one of the first to know, Sheriff. I promise.' With that, Will nodded once and walked calmly from the stables.

'I'm thinkin' you an' him get along real well,' Wale said to the buckskin. Then he swore, turned away and made his way back to the jailhouse.

The next morning, Cooter Lennon walked into the Beef 'n' Biscuit, for breakfast. He smiled brightly at the girl behind the counter. 'Mornin', Elodie.'

'Hi Cooter. Thick cut ham an' eggs?' the pretty girl said, returning his smile.

'Yeah, why not?' Cooter drawled. Plenty o' both.'

He glanced around, saw Will Sparrow sitting over by the front window, sipping coffee. He stared until Will became aware, then he dropped his gaze. When Elodie placed his meal in front of him, he thanked her, immediately picked up the plate and followed her back to the counter and climbed on to a stool. 'He's a moody sort o' feller. What do you make of him?' he asked quietly.

Elodie looked over at Will, frowned at Cooter. 'He looks dangerous, Cooter. But I can see loneliness. Have you noticed his eyes?'

'Yeah, I have . . . saw why he might be.'

Elodie nodded, took another sneaky look towards the window. It was then that Polk Chatham came through the front door. He spotted Will straight away, took a couple of paces to look down at him.

'Been lookin' for you,' he said.

'Someone warned me you might.'

'That's 'cause no one does that to me . . . no one.'

'Probably due to the company you keep. But I'll wager there's a few who've thought about it.'

Cooter came off his stool in a flash. 'Hold it right there, you two. There'll be none o' your trouble in here.'

'Stay out o' this, Deputy. This feller caught me cold last night, an' there's a price to pay,' Chatham rasped. 'I'll be waitin' outside, if you've the guts.'

'Mister, I'm not going anywhere until I've finished my coffee,' Will said softly. 'Now, do you mind

25

moving on before you curdle the cream.'

Cooter cursed them both and drew his gun. 'Outside, Chatham. Now,' he barked.

'There goes a man with little grasp of right and wrong,' Will started when Chatham had gone. 'If I thought he could read, I'd say he's been turned by those dime novels.'

Cooter looked crossly at Will. 'You keep sittin' there, Sparrow. Chatham might be the Ratsnake, but he's also handy with that gun of his.'

Will smiled tiredly and finished his coffee, picked up the empty cup and took it to the counter. 'That was a real fine breakfast, ma'am. I'll be back for lunch,' he said to Elodie. Then, without another word, he brushed past the confused, hapless deputy and walked out on to the boardwalk. 'He might not have done the words, but he's certainly looked at the pictures,' he muttered, looking eastwards.

Polk Chatham was standing in the middle of the street with the early-morning sun rising behind him.

Will stepped down from the boardwalk to the hard-packed dirt. He stood loose, facing Chatham with the sheriff's advice about backing down ringing in his ears. He didn't know the man and didn't want to kill him. But he didn't know how to get out of the situation other than being backshot.

Chatham assumed the typical, spread of legs, with his hand clawing, hovering just above his gun butt, stance.

'I've no interest in gunfighting you, Chatham,' Will called. 'Turn away now, before the spectators arrive. You'll save your life and some face.'

But Will realized his words were futile. '*Cut the crap an' shoot the bastard*,' was the legendary counsel that came to mind when he saw Chatham making his move.

It was a fast draw, the Colt coming up with an accurate bead on Will's chest. But Will knew when Chatham would pull his gun, even before Chatham himself did. His bullet took Chatham square on, neatly in the centre of his chest. The cowhand fired into the ground, then he twisted around, staggered sideways and fell.

Cooter tore past Will to kneel beside Chatham. He made a quick check, then stood to cover Will with his gun. 'Jailhouse time, Sparrow. Sheriff's goin' to want to talk to you. Probably me too,' he added miserably.

Will didn't seem to hold any expression on his face or in his eyes. 'He'd have been happier if I'd just died without putting up any sort of resistance. He told me as much.'

'Just put your goddamn gun away, and come with me,' Lennon almost snapped.

'He's done just like you told him not to, Sheriff,' Cooter called out as he ushered Will through the jailhouse door. 'He's shot an' killed Polk Chatham – Ratsnake.'

From his desk, Wale nodded, appearing calm. 'I heard the shootin' an' guessed. It was only a matter o' time. How'd it happen?'

Will took his hat off, bashed it against his knee as if to clear it of something. 'The man was in middle of the street waiting to shoot me. I waited as long as I could to make sure. Then I had to do something.'

'Yeah, course you did. Even though I'd told you to back down.'

'I'd already told him to leave me alone, god-damnit,' Will retorted. 'You'd rather it had been me? What would you have done then, Sheriff? Turned a blind eye because of this all-powerful Rochester man?'

Wale considered for a moment before choosing an answer. 'Is that right, Cooter? Did he tell Chatham to walk away?'

'I guess so. Not in so many words maybe, but the meanin' was there sure enough. He told him out there in the street . . . said he didn't want to kill him.'

'Hmm.' Wale looked more closely at Will, as though looking for signs of the truth.

'He went for his gun,' Will said. 'I don't think he wanted to show me a new trick he'd learned.'

'Well there's nothin' much I can do about it, then.' Wale issued a tight smile, grunted as though finishing a meal.

'What about the body? Are we goin' to do

28

anythin' about that?' Cooter asked.

'We can leave him out there for the night soilers. Either that or Sparrow can bury him. He killed him, after all. I ain't too fussy about graveside words for a ratsnake.'

'I'll do it. Seems the least I can do,' Will murmured.

'Then you shift off,' Wale barked. 'I'm lookin' forward to seein' your trail dust, feller.'

'When my business is done, Sheriff,' Will said as he headed for the door. 'That unlucky son-of-a-bitch wasn't it.'

Will stepped out into the sunshine, met the eyes of a few inquisitive townsfolk. Then he walked to Chatham's body, which was already attracting the interest of two mangy dogs and a boy with a switch.

Back in the jailhouse, Cooter was speaking to Wale. 'Hell, Ambrose, he's fast. Quicker'n you could see,' he said excitedly.

Wale folded his heavy hands on top of the desk. 'Yeah. It's usually the way bad news travels,' he replied, grimly.

5

The sun was high in the sky as Will turned away from Polk Chatham's grave. He walked back to the livery, handed back the shovel and hoe, then made his way to the Rugosa Saloon.

The barkeep served Will quickly and without any exchange or fuss, then watched him go to the table near the far corner.

As was his custom, Will sat with his back to the wall. He sipped his beer as a solitary man, but he was making a subtle study of every man who came through the swing doors.

Juno Hemsby entered, took a look around and saw Will. He strolled over, took a seat at the adjacent table and built himself a smoke. Will spared him a look and a nod, then concentrated on the batwings again.

'Polk Chatham was a loathsome being, even more so after a skinful. I wasn't there, but did you have to shoot him dead?' the deputy inquired.

Will turned slowly, settled his chilly gaze on Hemsby. 'If I hadn't, he was likely to sit right up and put a bullet between my shoulder blades when I walked off. That's the sort of loathsome being he was,' Will replied slowly.

'You make killin' someone sound like dispensin' with a pot chicken,' Hemsby said. 'You knew Wale didn't want you pullin' iron while you were in town.'

'I told him I'd defend myself if I had to. I reckon I had to.'

'Well,' Hemsby drawled, his features getting even tougher. 'If you're interested, I got one or two reasons of my own not to let that happen again. Namely, this here badge of office an' my Dragoon's Colt.'

'Mighty powerful arguments. Anything else you got to worry me with?'

'Yeah. Wale's real worried, an' given a chance he'll try an' stop you. I'm not for lettin' that happen. I owe him too much.'

Will offered a small smile of appreciation, which Hemsby returned. Then the deputy sheriff noticed that Will was suddenly looking elsewhere. He was watching two men who had come from a private alcove on the far side of the long bar. Hemsby audibly groaned with apprehension at the Mexican brothers, Felipe and Manuel Pinto.

The brothers spotted Will and smirked at each

other, sauntering over to stand a few feet from his table.

'*Saludo*, William Sparrow,' Felipe Pinto said. 'Long time. *Tiempo largo.*'

'Yeah, for all of us.' Will nodded, then at Manuel.

Hemsby snorted and coughed noisily for attention.

'*Buen día, Comisionado*,' Felipe teased in acknowledgment, then continued his exchange with Will. 'It was Alcalde,' he said.

'More than a year ago.'

'You were looking for three men, I remember.'

'*Sí,*' Will murmured picking up his beer and taking another sip.

'An' you kill a man here this morning.'

Will didn't answer, giving Felipe Pinto a lengthy stare instead.

Never being one to push his hand or overstay a welcome, Felipe bid his farewell. '*Otro momento,*' he said with a hollow smile, and the Pinto brothers walked directly from the saloon.

At once, Hemsby rounded on Will. 'So that's what you're doin' in Magdalena. You're after those three men.'

Will shook his head resignedly. 'Two. And to stop you asking, I caught up with one of them in somewhere called Dixon Valedo. He told me the others are here, or hereabouts.'

'What happened to him . . . the one you caught up with?'

'He died.'

'Yeah, lead poisonin' I bet. An' you're intendin' to kill the other two – here?'

'That was my intention.'

'I'm assumin' you got good reason. An' askin' as a lawman, how long you been chasin' 'em?' Hemsby pressed.

'Two years next week.'

For a moment, Hemsby fell to silent thinking. 'What about them Pintos? How come you know them?'

Will smiled. 'We had a run-in of sorts in Alcalde.'

'What was it about?'

'A girl, of course. Felipe was getting a bit heavy-handed in his billing an' cooing.'

'An' that's when you stepped in?'

'That's right. She didn't like it. I was doing my bit for law an' order.'

'An' they've got nothin' to do with you bein' in town?'

'No.'

'You know they're mercenaries . . . paid gun-slingers? They work for anyone who puts up.'

Will pushed up from the table. 'Yeah, I know who and what they are,' he said tolerantly. 'But every-body's got to be something, Deputy. It doesn't mean you're all bad . . . can't listen to reason. And you are asking too many questions.'

*

33

Cooter Lennon checked himself in the wall mirror. For the umpteenth time he straightened his necktie, moved the flat of his hand across his gleaming hair.

'How do I look?' he asked Wale.

The sheriff looked up from an old copy of the *Albuquerque Tribune*. 'You look just fine, Cooter. Same as the last time you asked. But any more o' that musk oil, an' I'll be forced to sit out in the street.'

Cooter beamed. 'An' you're sure you won't be needin' me tonight?'

'Put it like this. There's someone needs you more. Besides, if I said I did, you'd most likely hold it against me for the rest o' your natural. I couldn't live with that. Now, go take Elodie to the dance. Juno an' me'll take care of anythin' that happens here.'

Cooter still hesitated. 'Well, you know where I'll be – just a holler away.'

'If you're not out o' this office in five minutes, I'll lock you up for loiterin'. Now git,' Wale said gruffly.

Cooter was still grinning as he hopped lightly on to the boardwalk. He headed west up the main street, then the short distance on to the Wesker house. He vaulted the picket fence, walked briskly to the front door and knocked firmly. He pulled off his hat, twirled the brim in his hands and waited. Presently, the door opened and a wedge of yellow light lit the front of his store-bought suit.

'Evenin', Mrs Wesker,' he greeted with a friendly grin.

'Elodie's not quite ready, Cooter. Come on in.'

The young lawman stepped inside and Mrs Wesker led the way into the house.

On the first Saturday of every month, the people of Magdalena held a dance night. For the older folk, it was a welcome break from the dullness and rigour of their work; for the youngsters, a chance to mingle and strut their full-blooded stuff.

After a ten-minute wait, Elodie came down the hall to the parlour, where she gave a self-conscious twirl in the centre of the floor. 'Do you like it?' she said, smiling happily at Cooter.

'Sure do,' he replied in admiration. 'That didn't come from the mercantile, I know. You were always goin' to be the best lookin' but now you're the best turned out as well.'

'I'm glad you approve, Cooter. But everybody knows that Mr Rochester's niece will be both those things. She always is.'

Cooter reached out and took her small hand in his. 'Not in my book,' he said. 'An' I reckon that modesty is the sweetest o' songbirds.'

Elodie's mother smiled at them. 'Go and have a good time. Mr Wesker and I will be close behind you.'

'We're not going to be late, are we?' Elodie asked

as Cooter opened the front gate. 'Everybody looks at you just so, and we don't want to miss that first dance.'

'I'm not missin' anything, Elodie.' Cooter slipped his arm through hers, and they started their walk towards the dance hall at the other end of town.

Once past the Beef 'n' Biscuit, they saw that a crowd was already tailing back. Others were arriving on horseback, buggies and other assorted vehicles.

Outside the jailhouse, Juno Hemsby had his foot up on the railing. He appeared to be casually watching the to and fro. 'Handsome pair,' he murmured, casually flicking the dead end of a smoke into the street. 'Best keep your eyes an' ears open tonight, Miss Elodie. The boy's seriously dressed for somethin'.'

'Why don't you go back in an' torment the sheriff, Juno? It's not funny any more,' Cooter railed.

Elodie laughed quietly at Cooter's discomfort. But sensed the change in his tone. 'Isn't that the young man that was in trouble earlier? What was his name . . . Sparrow?' she said, breaking the obvious strain.

Cooter and Hemsby turned to look at the figure across the street. Will Sparrow was standing quietly in deeper shadow, but he'd been walking away from the dance hall.

'Ma'am.' Hemsby touched his hat, then walked

off across the street.

'Well now,' he said as he approached Will Sparrow. 'If you're goin' to cut a rug tonight, you're headed in the wrong direction.'

'You sound as if you care,' Will replied. 'Unless that's your way of extendin' me an invite.'

Hemsby's eyes hardened. 'No – to both. You mind tellin' me where you are goin'?'

Will held the deputy's intimidating stare. 'How many more times? You know why I'm here . . . that I want no interference from you or any other badge-toting do-gooder,' he declared. For a moment, Will wondered whether Hemsby, like Polk Chatham, had been drinking, his spleen livened by cheap whiskey. But he decided he didn't care much, and without another word continued on his way to the Rugosa Saloon.

Hemsby watched until Will disappeared among townsfolk mingling on the boardwalk, into the darkness. Then he flinched, gulped when a hand touched him on the shoulder.

'Damn an' blast, Cooter. Don't go doin' that. Not in the goddamn dark.'

'He got you on edge too, Juno?'

'Yeah. Him an' them like him,' Hemsby muttered, looking uneasy.

A handful of riders drew up close to the dance hall, turning their mounts, looking around them in all directions. They were closely followed by a fancy

37

black Dearborn, that carried Farley Rochester and his niece, Rose. The rancher helped the girl down, then handed the rig over to one of his men to take care of. With relaxed smiles, the pair went up the short flight of steps together, through the open, welcoming doors of the dance hall.

6

Will didn't go into the saloon. Instead, he sat on one of the deckchairs, beneath the overhang. He tugged the brim of his hat to cover his forehead and half closed his eyes. He was listening to the musical strains drifting from the dance hall when the saloon doors alongside him burst open. He cursed and pulled his hat down further when Felipe and Manuel Pinto reeled out on to the boardwalk, stumbling down to the street. He heard Manuel's weird, grating laugh as they lumbered drunkenly up towards the dance hall in search of more entertainment.

It didn't take long for Will to figure that that was where he should be. The men he sought might just seek the anonymous throng of noise and movement if they came to Magdalena. He retraced his steps but saw no sign of anyone or anything resembling trouble. He stood outside the hall for a moment, almost tapped his foot to the lively strain of a two-step, then he took a deep breath and stepped inside.

His grey eyes searched the milling twirl of faces, flicking over the crowded dance floor. He had a quick look at the group of men who stood at the punch bowl, holding for a second when he noticed Rose Rochester.

'No guns in here, mister,' a townsman said, walking towards him. 'If you're stayin' peg your gunbelt with the others.'

Will shook his head slightly. 'I'm not. I'm just having a look,' he replied.

The man nodded, gave Will an old-fashioned look, and moved on to officiate elsewhere.

Elodie Wesker saw Will. She said something quickly to her mother, then crossed the floor in a flurry of skirts, to stand diffidently in front of him.

It's Mr Sparrow, isn't it? Our small town's latest event,' she murmured. 'Why don't you come on in and enjoy yourself?'

Will touched the brim of his hat. 'I reckon *event*'s a tad strong, ma'am. As for me not coming in, there's good enough reasons. Not being able to dance is one of 'em.'

Elodie smiled charmingly. 'Why, I'm sure there's enough of us here to teach you. Most of the time it's putting one foot in front of another and turning about. You can manage that, can't you?'

A faint smile moved the corners of Will's mouth. 'There's a bar in Alcalde with a sign that says, "When you dance, take heed who you take by the hand". I think it's more than a reminder to strangers.'

Well, if it's some sort of warning, who's here tonight who's likely to worry *you*, Mr Sparrow?'

'I'd say that deputy lawman friend of yours. The one you came in with who's giving us both a mean look. But maybe there's someone else,' Will added. 'For example, that feller wearing the beaver hat standing by the punch bowl. Do you know him?'

Elodie looked, turned back. 'Of course. That's Cyrus Oldring of the O Ring.'

'He looks like he might own it.'

'He does. For a few years. Why him?'

'No reason,' Will said quietly. 'For a moment I thought I knew him.'

'Oh well, if you're not coming in, Mr Sparrow, I won't keep you. Goodnight.'

Will smiled and said goodnight. 'Whoever you are,' he said under his breath.

Ambrose Wale rubbed a hand wearily over his face, then stood up. He buttoned his tattered Mackinaw, dragged his hat down firmly and picked up his shotgun. He listened for a moment, then opened and closed the jailhouse door quietly. From the boardwalk, his perceptive eyes scanned the length of the lantern-lit street. He sensed trouble this night, with a mix of townsfolk, cowhands and leather-slappers drinking and dancing under one roof. In his experience, it was a heady brew, neither friendly nor long-lasting.

The sheriff stepped from the boardwalk to the hard-runnelled dust of the main street, cutting a long and steady diagonal path along to the Rugosa Saloon.

From the establishment's batwings, there appeared to be only two customers: a drunken towner and Will Sparrow. The drunk didn't bother to raise his face and Wale disregarded him, just nodded at Cato as he walked unhurriedly to Will's table.

'Decided not to go gunnin' for any Rochester cowboys, then? Seein' as they'll all likely be in one place,' he said.

'Why should I be doing that, Sheriff?' Will replied. 'They're not the ones giving me grief . . . disturbing my peace.'

The sheriff sniffed. 'Two weeks ago, Sparrow, this town was quiet an' peaceable. Now, gunfighters are walkin' the streets as if there's a goddamn convention. Some I know are cold-blooded killers, but until they break the law, I can't touch 'em. All I can do is get on their backs an' disturb *their* peace. You understand?'

'Yeah, I understand. So why not do it? Tell *them* to

ride on, like you keep telling *me*,' Will said drily.

'I would, goddamnit, but Addison Rugosa has given 'em work. What about you? How the hell are you payin' your way?'

'I'm a man of independent means, Sheriff. Last time I heard, that wasn't a crime,' Will answered coolly. He was wondering when the sheriff was going to ask about the men he'd trailed to Magdalena. *Juno Hemsby must have told you by now,* he was thinking.

As Wale was about to respond, a chubby youngster pushed excitedly through the doors. 'Sheriff, you best get to the dance. There's goin' to be trouble,' he blurted.

'Calm down, Sam. What kind o' trouble?' Wale asked.

Sam licked his dry lips, had a cautious glance at Will. 'It's your deputy, Cooter. He's in trouble with a Mex.'

Will groaned in acknowledgment, and the chub gave him another glance. 'Seems this Mex was tryin' to horn in an' make somethin' with Miss Elodie, an' Cooter didn't like it. They swung a few punches, but the Mex could hardly stand he was so full o' liquor.'

'Where's the trouble, then, Sam? Sounds to me like it's over.'

'No no. Cooter got the best of it, but the Mex said for him to get a gun an' settle it proper.'

'Where is he now?'

'Still there waitin', an' I think there's two of 'em.'

'No, Cooter. Where's Cooter?'

'Over at the jailhouse, I guess. You best do somethin', Sheriff.'

Wale swore colourfully. 'Sparrow, instead of sittin' here twiddlin' your thumbs, make yourself useful. Head over to the jail an'—'

'I'm not heading anywhere, Sheriff,' Will replied abruptly with a tight smile and a shake of his head. 'You're mistaking me for one of your deputies, an' *that I ain't.* I'm staying right here away from trouble.'

Wale glared at Will for a moment, then with fat Sam puffing close behind, he strode huffily from the saloon.

Will told himself it was none of his business. Felipe Pinto was forever in trouble with girls and the law. It was his problem, and he wouldn't want it any other way. But, on the premise that you never knew what kind of person was attracted to a gun-fight, Will had another thought, and decided to go take a look.

7

There was a big crowd outside the dance hall, most of them local townsfolk. Felipe Pinto was standing away to one side almost in the centre of the street and arguing fiercely with Addison Riggs. Elodie was looking worried and frightened, standing close to her folks.

A bunch of Rochester riders lined the walk in front of the big hall; Will thought that most of them looked like hired guns. The rancher and his niece stood just inside the hall, watching.

Ambrose Wale stepped into the light thrown across the street from the hall. He was less than ten paces from Pinto when he raised the slant of his shotgun.

'I gave you a warnin' when you rode in, Pinto. I told to keep out o' trouble,' he rasped. 'Now, Cooter Lennon tells me you've been pawin' Elodie Wesker – forcin' yourself on her against her will.

What do you say?'

'I say, your young deputy is mistaken, Sheriff. Ask the lady. You arrest me for being bold and handsome. Maybe dangerous?'

'I'm takin' you in for lewd behaviour an' causin' a breach o' the peace,' Wale returned flatly. 'Now, drop your hardware an' come real quiet.'

'Ahh, good Sheriff. If I decide no, I can shoot an' kill you before you move an inch.'

'That would be risky.' Wale inclined his head slightly for effect. 'You're drunk, Pinto, but not enough to take chances,' he said. 'This brute could take down you an' half that building across the street. You want to risk it?'

While Pinto was estimating Wale's challenge, another of Riggs's workers stepped forward.

But Juno Hemsby had seen the man move. 'Best if you stay out o' this, Ventress,' he advised, easing himself away from a corral corner post. 'If you don't want one o' my big bullets in the back of your head.'

The man named Ventress cursed, unable to see Hemsby, whose voice came from the darkness behind him. But what he also couldn't see and didn't know was that Manuel Pinto was ramming the barrel of his Colt into the middle of Hemsby's back. All he could hear was the Mexican's throaty crackle of a laugh.

'Where's the *muchacho*, Sheriff?' Felipe Pinto asked. 'Frightened of dark, maybe?'

'He's coolin' down . . . kickin' his heels in the jail-house,' Wale said stiffly. 'Why don't you come with me an' do the same before someone gets hurt?'

'There's only *one* person likely to get hurt,' Ventress threatened.

The hostile language and one-sidedness was enough for Will. *Just stay out of trouble*, he told himself as he walked up to stand beside Wale. *It's none of your business.*

'What are you doing, Will Sparrow? This is nothing to you,' Felipe Pinto growled as if reading Will's thoughts.

Will smiled coldly. 'It's the odds. I like them more even; it's a weakness of mine.'

A vicious gleam entered Pinto's dark eyes. 'A weakness to get you killed, *amigo.*'

'Yeah, this is nothin' to do with him, Pinto,' Wale chimed in. 'Back off, feller, it ain't your fight,' he then snarled at Will. 'You told me that much just now.'

'This man doesn't hold up to authority or people. He'll kill you in a blink. And if *he* doesn't, his *brother* will,' Will replied as calmly as he could. 'Dying with your boots on, Sheriff, really ain't that heroic.'

'It wasn't me wanted out, goddamnit. You said—' the sheriff started to say, but Will interrupted him.

'When it starts, just shoot Ventress,' he rasped stubbornly.

Juno Hemsby could do nothing more than watch,

feeling his vitals pinch at the thought of a bullet in the spine. But he realized the mute Mexican would have to back off and he smiled bleakly into the darkness.

When the Pintos fanned out, Will didn't move, just stood calm and loose.

'OK, Will Sparrow, see you in hell,' Felipe Pinto called a moment later.

Both men dashed their gun hands to their Colts. Pinto was fast and going to be accurate, but it was Will's bullet that hit home.

Ventress fired, too, the bullet thumping into the meat of Wale's shoulder, knocking him, kneeling, to the ground. But a moment later, Wale's own shotgun detonated with a thunderous roar, the blast hurling Ventress's lifeless body several paces across the hard-packed dirt.

With a bullet in the chest, Felipe Pinto was still on his feet, swinging his gun up for another shot. Will grimaced, cursing as he added another bullet to the same spot.

Pinto's legs buckled. 'I'll get there,' he seethed, as he fell on his back. He looked up blindly, gave one last convulsive kick before lying still.

No one spoke, hardly moved except for Will, who straightened up from the crouch he'd dropped into. Folk started to crowd the sheriff, taking a closer look at the two dead men, snorting at the pall of burnt cordite.

Hemsby stepped away from Manuel Pinto. 'We ain't finished, Mex. But you're as good as dead,' he rasped and hurried over to kneel beside Wale.

'Get the doc out here,' he bellowed.

'I already am,' a tall, thin man carrying a Gladstone bag replied coolly. 'I hadn't planned for a quiet night in.'

Then the attention moved on to Will, who, carefully, backed away. He was making an attempt at being unnoticed, wandering casually back down to the saloon.

Later, when Juno Hemsby shoved open the doors of the saloon, he saw Will seated at his usual table.

'Sheriff wants to see you,' he called out plainly. 'He's at home.'

'Well, you go and tell him, I'm at the Rugosa Saloon having a beer,' came Will's mellow reply.

'He's dark-mooded, Sparrow. Said I was to persuade if I had to,' Hemsby snapped, then misguidedly placed his hand on the butt of his big Dragoon's Colt.

'Easy, feller. He ain't worth being one-legged for.' Will spoke with a tolerant shake of his head, and Hemsby froze at the unmistakeable click of a Colt revolver being actioned from under the tabletop. 'There's some who can pull a trigger to kill, and some who can't,' Will continued. 'Which one are you, Hemsby?'

'There must be pure snake blood runnin' through you,' Hemsby breathed.

'No. But I might have been taught by one.'

'Your pa didn't teach you?'

'No. His foreman. My pa's dead.'

'I'm sorry. He figured in your life did he . . . the foreman?'

'Yeah, still does . . . is doing right now. He's Copperhead Joad. You might have heard of him.'

Hemsby's eyes narrowed in concentration. 'Copperhead Joad,' he repeated. 'Didn't he ride with McNelly's Raiders or some such border outfit? I seem to recollect a bushwhacker took him out along the Nueces Strip. It was a few years back.'

'Well, that's what we had the world and his dog believe,' Will granted. 'But he was backshot. The chicken liver ran all the way to El Paso.'

Hemsby lifted his chin. 'Don't tell me. There was another fatal case o' lead poisonin'? So what did happen to Joad?'

'My pa bound him up best he could and brought him back to the ranch. He's been there ever since. That was ten years ago.'

'An' it was *him* taught you when an' when not to use a gun, huh?' Hemsby asked. But when he saw the look in Will's eye, the grind of his jaw, he knew there'd be no more conversation.

'Right. So you'll be seein' the sheriff in a while . . . a short while? I'll take a seat outside in the

50

meantime,' he said.

Will waited until the deputy had walked from the saloon, then he slowly came to his feet. He'd been watching a cowhand who had come in a little earlier with three other men. He drained his glass, then stepped over to where they were standing at the bar.

The barkeep, Cato, watched him nervously. He knew of Will's ability with a gun, was thankful he'd got off lightly for riling him the other night.

'Another beer, Will . . . Mr Sparrow? Perhaps a glass of honest whiskey?' he asked amiably.

Will ignored him. 'Are you working for Rochester?' he asked of the cowhand.

'That's right. What's it got to do with you?' the man replied brusquely.

'Nothing. But I would like to ask you a question.'

'Go ahead.'

Will paused, as if it were him considering an option from the cowboy. 'Have you come across someone going by the name of Patch, Oliver Patch?' he asked.

Giving Will a thoughtful look, the cowboy sniffed and tugged his nose. 'Can't say I have, no. Not the sort of handle you forget, is it?'

Will matched the man's stare. 'Not for me it's not. I just wondered. Perhaps your friends here?' he hinted, but the other men shook their heads.

'What do you want him for?' the first cowboy asked. 'If I ever run into him, I'll mention it.'

'Thanks, but no need. I'm also on the lookout for a moon-eyed feller – Toll Judkins. I don't suppose you've crossed his trail either?'

'Look, feller we came in here for a drink, not to run through your wanted list,' the cowboy said. 'Unless there's rewards for these fellers, go ask someone else.'

Will allowed each man a short, chilly glance, then he offered his thanks, nodded at Cato and walked straight from the saloon.

8

Will stepped out on to the saloon porch to stand beside Hemsby. He leaned a shoulder against a support, looked up and down the street into the darkness.

'That stuff I was telling you earlier,' he started. 'Well that was strictly 'tween you and me. Any further, and you know what happens.'

'Yeah. Somethin' unpleasant, I guess.'

'Our little town hop got broken up, then?'

Hemsby nodded. 'Yeah. I guess everythin' fell a bit flat after the shootin' an' all.'

'Too bad. You can't have everything, Deputy. Do you want me to visit your boss now?'

'I did ten minutes ago, but as you say, you can't. . . .' Hemsby went off muttering, leading the way down the main street to the western end of town. Not far from where Elodie Wesker lived, they turned into a neat, narrow-fronted dwelling with a simple front yard. At the door, Hemsby knocked, removing his hat at the same time.

The door was opened by a slight girl of about eighteen years. Her appearance took Will by surprise. Her skin was dark and her eyes were almost as black as her long, straight hair.

'Evenin', Miss Laurel. That tetchy pa of yours still awake?' Hemsby greeted.

'Yes, Juno, he is, and screaming for all sorts of your anatomy. He's on the parlour couch,' the girl replied.

Will followed Hemsby into the house. He nodded politely, a little uncomfortably, as Laurel Wale stood aside, closing the door behind him.

Hemsby smiled uneasily at the injured sheriff. 'How's the wound?' he asked.

'Crossed the Rio Grande to get him, did you?' Wale snorted back.

'I had a little business to attend to,' Will cut in. 'Something on your mind, Sheriff?'

'Yeah, there is. An' you can take off that blasted hat. Laurel, you go make us a pot o' coffee.'

Laurel put out a small hand. 'I'm Laurel Wale,' she said to Will.

'Pleased to meet you, Laurel. Real pleased. I'm Will Sparrow,' he said sincerely, taking her hand in an enthusiastic grip.

'Why'd you back me up tonight?' Wale asked, grunting as pain shot through his shoulder.

Will was still smiling as Laurel left the room, but he turned his attention back to the sheriff. 'Haven't quite figured that myself yet. But a friend once told me that, if you surprise your enemy, he's half beat,' he answered quietly.

'It don't answer my question, but I take it you mean the Pinto brothers,' Wale grated back. 'When I saw you ride into town, Sparrow, I pegged you straight off as trouble – gun trouble. Do you want to try an' change that view?'

'With respect, Sheriff, an' this being your home an' all, I don't see why.'

'What you mean is, you got stuff to say that might upset my daughter if she was in the room,' Wale went on. 'Well she ain't, goddamnit, so tell me why you ain't signed on with Addison Riggs? All the others have, so why not you?'

'He sure offered. But I've got securities. I already told you that.'

'Where'd you get money, unless it was for a hired gun?'

'That's a cheeky question, Mr Wale, even for a sheriff who hasn't got an innocent daughter standing beside him,' Will smiled out his reply. 'But I'll tell you anyway. I've got a ranch up in Colorado. When I need funds, I wire my foreman.'

Wale suddenly showed more interest. 'I know something of the land this side o' the Arkansas. Whereabouts?'

'The San Louis Valley.'

'So how many head you runnin'?' Hemsby chipped in, using the protection of Wale's interest to draw out more information.

'I don't know for sure. Three thousand, maybe.'

'Maybe?' Wale queried. 'Don't you know?'

'No. I'm the rancher, not a tally hand. What the hell's this got to do with you, anyhow?' Will retorted.

Wale grunted again. He rested his head back against the couch, his brows knitting together in concern. 'I'm sorry, Sparrow,' he said after a long pause. 'You more'n likely saved my life out there tonight. I guess I'm tryin' to figure out why an' goin' the wrong way about it ... askin' the wrong questions. Maybe I should offer you a job? I look like bein' laid up here for some time.'

Will ran his fingers through his hair. 'Right now, the coffee will be just fine,' he said, his smile returning as Laurel came back through the door.

Laurel told them it would be a few more minutes before the coffee was ready, and sat back down in her chair. She was fascinated by Will, the grey eyes that held some humour, his unusual, quietly spoken manner. He appeared to be at ease, yet she sensed he could spring at the drop of a hat.

'You won't even consider my offer?' Wale asked.

'No need. I'll thank you for making it, though.'

'What'll you do now?'

'Go back to my room and get my head down, for a start.'

'Yeah, an' that goes for you, too, Ambrose,' Hemsby said as he stood up.

Laurel did the same, going to her father and pulling the blanket higher over his chest. 'Juno's right, Pa. You rest up now. Talk to Mr Sparrow some other time.'

Wale muttered an acknowledgment. 'If you were thinkin' of leavin' town, I suggest you don't, Will Sparrow,' he advised.

'Promise I'll stop by. Meantime it's goodnight to you all,' he said. Then he walked to the door, replacing his hat as he went out.

When he was at the gate, Laurel called to him. 'Mr Sparrow. May I speak with you a moment?'

Will quickly said yes, waiting a few moments for Hemsby to go past, to stand a short distance along the street in the deeper shadow.

'Yes, ma'am,' he replied. 'If you're wanting to know why I'm not staying for the coffee, I—'

'No, it's not that,' Laurel interrupted, standing closer to him than she had in the house. 'I wanted to thank you for what you did tonight . . . saving my pa's life.'

'At the time I was saving the sheriff's life. Discovering it was your pa makes it even more worthwhile.'

Laurel tried to see Will's eyes but it was too dark

to see clearly. 'You don't have any family, Mr Sparrow?'

'No, ma'am. My pa was shot dead a few years ago. Before that, my ma ran off with a cowboy, and I've not heard from her since. My foreman's the only real friend I have. That's OK with me, though.'

They stood in silence for a time, Lauren fiddling with a silver beaded bracelet on her left wrist.

'Did you go to the dance tonight? I didn't see you there,' Will said.

'Pa said I was to, but no I didn't go.' Laurel lowered her head, rubbing at a blue bead with her thumb. 'Did you go?' she countered.

'Sort of. I don't dance . . . just stood at the door listening, tapping my toe for a few moments. That was when other events sort of took over. Can I say something, Miss Laurel?' he said on a different note. 'I've been looking forward to going home but, well, ever since meeting you – what, fifteen minutes ago – I'm suddenly not in such a hurry any more, and that's the strange truth of it.'

'Heavens above, Mr Sparrow,' Laurel responded with an almost audible gasp. 'Your quiet manner is sure wrapping up something else.'

'Don't think too badly of me because of it, Laurel. It's an honest parcel.'

They lapsed into a thoughtful silence again, but this time it was shattered by the blast of a rifle from across the street. The bullet pulsed close to Will's face, smashing into the timber cladding of the Wale home.

Reacting instantly, Will leapt on Laurel, dragging her to the ground, and pulled her roughly over by the low fence. He then drew his Colt and actioned it.

The rifle crashed out again, splitting the darkness, sending splinters of a fence paling to shower over them. But this time, Will saw the flash from the alley opposite, where he'd guessed it was. His two quick returning shots were accompanied by the boom of a big Dragoon's Colt from down the street.

'Laurel? Laurel, are you OK?' Hemsby yelled anxiously.

'Yeah, she's fine. We both are,' Will replied, feeling the warmth of her body under his protective left arm. 'You stay here until it's safe to get inside, OK?' he added quietly.

'Yes, OK,' she murmured huskily, watching him roll towards the gate.

The rifle blasted again, echoed by Hemsby's Colt. Will ran diagonally across the street until he reached a storefront not far from Baxter's Mercantile.

Hemsby had made it to the same side of the street, the far side of the alley mouth. If anyone should emerge from the dark maw of the alley, it would put them in the close, lethal crossfire of both Hemsby's and Will's guns.

Will edged to the corner of the building, was almost there when he heard the dull sound of running feet. He stepped forward, sending two searching shots down the alley, then Hemsby was there, peering intently into the darkness.

'Think you got him?' the deputy hissed.

'Don't know. Only one way to find out.' Will started off down the alley, with Hemsby siding to his left. But when they reached the end of the run, they had seen and heard nothing, except the troubled barking of Mose Baxter's watchdog.

'Well, he sure didn't get past us,' Hemsby said. 'Who do you think it was? Maybe one o' them fellers you're after,' he continued when Will didn't respond. 'Maybe they heard you was in town an' figured they'd get you afore you got them.'

'Yeah, maybe,' Will answered quietly and distractedly, but his voice was measured anger. 'Two of those shots were real close to Laurel. That's bad,' he added a moment later. 'Let's get back.'

Across at the Wale house, Laurel had turned down the hall lamps, was standing behind the half-closed door.

'I don't know for sure that that was to do with me, Laurel, but I'm real sorry for it happening,' Will apologized.

'I'm a sheriff's daughter. It comes with the territory. For you, it's becoming a habit . . . saving us Wales.'

'But it shouldn't be in your front yard. I'd best get a move on. Goodnight.' Will nodded, turned and walked briskly back to the jailhouse with Hemsby.

'Perhaps I should have stayed for coffee after all,' he said, pouring himself a cup of tepid water from the desk pitcher. 'You haven't told Wale why I'm in Magdalena. How come?' he asked.

Hemsby was sitting at Ambrose Wale's desk, thoughtfully watching Will. 'Guess I plain forgot,' he replied. 'Besides, it's none of his business.'

'Did you forget to tell him about my foreman, as well?'

'That's nothin' to do with him, either.'

Will leaned down, looking Hemsby straight in the eye. 'I reckon it's more to do with knowing what I'd do if you'd said anything. Copperhead Joad has been known for ten years as Rufus Joad, and I'd react real bad if that was to get leaked. You'll sleep a lot easier just remembering that, Deputy.'

'If he doesn't ride into town causin' trouble, his secret's safe enough with me,' Hemsby huffed.

'That's good.' Will carefully placed the cup on top of the water pitcher and moved to the door. 'Goddamn good,' he confirmed, stepping back out to the boardwalk.

9

Early next morning, Will stirred, stretched and rolled from the bed, which he'd pulled to the far wall of the room. He made the bed, considered shaving and then put on a fresh shirt from his saddle-bag. He spent some time cleaning and reloading his Colt, then he left the room, going out to the Beef 'n' Biscuit for breakfast.

Fifteen minutes later Elodie Wesker placed ham and eggs, frijoles and black coffee in front of him, fussing with the cutlery while he patiently waited for her to finish.

'I bet these fixings are best when eaten still warm. What do you reckon?' he said with a mischievous grin.

'Sorry, I was just making the place look nice,' Elodie answered back. 'Will there be anything else, Mr Sparrow?'

'No. I reckon I've got most of it here. Maybe

more coffee. Thank you.'

Elodie started to say something further, but changed her mind and walked back to the kitchen.

Will ate his meal slowly, lifting his head occasionally to look out at the street.

He left a dollar dividend, then left the eatery to stand on the boardwalk. Townsfolk had started to move around, most of them dressed in their Sunday church clothes. Some nodded neutrally, some with distaste as they passed by; most just stared at him with open curiosity. Will guessed it was because, as Wale had done, they all thought he was some sort of hired gunman. He stared back and considered the infantile act of tongue-poking, but instead he shrugged tolerantly and walked on down to the livery.

He saddled his buckskin mare, mounted up and rode at a leisurely pace along the main street. But once out of the east end of town he turned to the north trail and let the horse have its head.

Powerful and energetic, the mare ate up ground for a few miles, and when Will eased it down to a slow canter it snorted disdainfully. But Will rode that way until he came to the creek where he'd crossed on first approaching Magdalena.

Laurel Wale was wearing a plaid shirt with the sleeves rolled up, and a green riding skirt. Her riding boots showed a film of dust and a felt hat was hanging down her back on a rawhide thong. She was standing by her bay mare while it drank.

She turned when she heard the rider approaching, her dark, oval features breaking into a genuine smile the moment she recognized Will. But it tightened when she saw the puzzled look across his face.

Will nodded as he reined in. Then he dismounted and led his horse to the water. It was shallow and pebble-bedded, about forty feet wide and clear running.

'Sheriff laying there with half his body shot away, and his daughter out skylarking,' he said without looking up.

'He hasn't got half of anything shot away and you know it, Will Sparrow,' she replied with another smile. 'Fact is, Doc Cotton and his wife kindly offered to spend a few hours with him. They all know I go for a ride most mornings, so today that's what he prescribed. Doctor's orders. And furthermore, my father is as tough as rawhide – tougher. He collects these injuries like badges of office.'

Will looked up. 'Yeah, that's what I was thinking,' he said, his eyes softening. 'He must be in good hands.'

'He is. I thank you for your concern, and good morning to you too.'

Will knelt, selected a stone from the water's edge and skimmed it across the surface of the water.

Laurel moved over to stand directly behind him.

'Father used to do that. He called it ducks an' drakes. He could reach the other side with a good stone,' she said. 'Can I ask why you're out here?'

'Because it means not being in town. Is that reason enough?'

'Yes it is, and something we've got in common,' she said, stepping back a few paces to sit on a grassy hummock. 'You're not married, are you?' she asked after a moment.

'After what I said to you yesternight? It's not likely, is it. Being married's something I'm keeping at arm's length. My ma, her name was Alma, she brought Pa nothing but misery. Once he found her in the hayloft with someone. He let her stay, though . . . for more cheating and lying. Huh; he gave her a lot more rope than the hired got, I can tell you. But one morning she was gone, taken up with a go-getting hand cowpoke. It was the last we ever saw or heard from her.'

Laurel dropped her chin, looked down at her hands. 'I'm sorry. I was only wondering. Like you, there was things running around in my head. What you told me made me feel warmer inside, kind and more vital than a dutiful daughter.'

'Good,' Will said. 'I was worried at first, but then I felt, *what the hell*. It was the truth.'

'As we're on such intimate terms now, I'm going to call you Will. So what's your ranch like? Tell me about it.'

Will moved towards her, sitting down on the twisted bole of a live oak, tipping his hat back. 'My pa named it Wolf Run. It's big now, and fine cattle country. There's a stream cuts it and never runs dry, even in the worst of droughts. Do you want to hear more?'

'Yes. That's not much,' Laurel said.

'Pa built it on his own – the cabin, rope corrals and a couple of lean-tos. Things were good for a while, then he went into the army, the cavalry, for two years. Ma said we should stay and take care of things, wait for him to come home. When he did, we worked hard. I was bigger by then and we took on a couple of extra hands. I'm getting to the meat of the tale; shall I go on?' he asked.

'Of course. You can't stop now.'

'We built the barn first, and after Ma ran out on us, we put up the bunkhouse. Pa bought more cattle and a year later we started on the main house. We went without when we had to, and over the years we expanded. Pa bought out a smaller spread and some nesters until we had one of the biggest spreads in the San Louis Valley.'

'So why are you here now, and not at home where you so obviously long to be?' Laurel asked huskily.

'Who was your mother?' was Will's answer.

'You're asking because of the way I look?'

'I guess so. And that beautiful piece of jewellery you wear.'

66

'She was Zuni – worked for the Agency,' Laurel said, touching her wristband as she spoke.

'Hmm. That's good. She must have been a smart lady.'

'Yes, she was. Thank you. But did no one ever advise you not to answer a question with another one?'

'No. It's been two years since I've been home,' he said. He continued: 'When Pa was in the army he was tried for treason. They alleged he'd caused the death of a whole troop by informing on their mission. He didn't, of course, and the court found him innocent of all charges. But there were some who believed he was guilty.'

'What happened? Tell me, Will. I'd like to hear the rest of the story.'

Will thought back, then went on. 'I was in our barn saddling horses, and I heard some riders come into our yard and pull up. Pa came out of the house and called them by name. But they just fired . . . emptied their guns into him. I ran out and they rode off. There were three of them. That's it, Laurel . . . and about how long it took.'

Will stood up, continued his story as Laurel sat watching him in silence. 'I buried my pa, then got our foreman to teach me how to use a gun. I spent months learning, practising, before I was good enough, then I rode away. I knew who the men were, you see.'

Will's eyes glinted cold. 'I found one of them some time back. He told me about the other two . . . where they were likely to be. I think that answers why I'm here.'

10

Laurel tried very hard to hold back her feeling of compassion, maybe a tear. She sat quietly, not doing or saying anything. She understood, but didn't know if there was a side to take.

It was in the affecting moments of silence that Will heard the light drumming of hoofs. Then he heard the horses nicker anxiously and he cursed. He looked across the creek at the riders, who were breaking through the stand of gnarled oaks and low bankside scrub. Four of them clipped into the water, reining in halfway across the shallows.

'This is Rochester land, mister. What's your business on it?' one of them shouted.

Will studied the riders, seeing and knowing instantly that none of them were the men he was looking for. 'I'm not doing much more than breathing at the moment, feller,' he said. 'He owns the air too, does he, this Rochester?'

'Howdy, Miss Wale,' the man said, disregarding Will. 'Mr Rochester knows you ride out this way to the stream. You're welcome anytime.'

'Yeah. Mornin', Miss Wale,' another rider joined in.

'The boss don't like trespassers on his land, mister. So you best get back on that buckskin an' dig your heels,' the first man continued.

Will shrugged and started for his horse. Being a ranch owner himself, he accepted Rochester's standing orders to his riders. He was about to ask Laurel if she'd be all right when another of the cowhands called out.

'Ain't you the sumbitch who cut down our own Ratsnake, Polk Chatham?'

Will turned to look at the man who'd spoken, saw that he was heavily built, darkly bearded and sat astride a dun mare.

'Yeah, this is him all right,' the deep, rough voice accepted. 'We all heard you're pretty handy with that Colt o' yours. I'm wonderin' how good you are without it.' The man looked around at his cronies, who started to guffaw and spit at the stream.

'Don't go scarin' the boy, Gordo,' someone called out. 'How'd it look to Miss Laurel with him gettin' his hands an' face all messed up?'

With more coarse laughter ringing out across the

stream, Will knew the Rochester cowboys weren't going to let him ride away and he cursed. 'Have another breakfast. I'll be a few more minutes,' he said, pushing his horse away.

The big man growled aggressively, climbed down from his mare and waded through the shallow water towards Will.

'Please don't fight,' Laurel asked of them. 'There's no need.'

Gordo stretched his neck, shoving his rough face closer to Will. 'Take a gunny's gun away, an' what you got?' he rasped.

Will unbuckled his gunbelt and handed it up to Laurel. 'Sorry, Laurel. Telling him there's no need to fight is *not* going to work.'

Laurel took the rig. As she did so, she couldn't help noticing the initials C.J. branded into the back of the holster.

Gordo grinned, ripping his own belt from his thick waist and tossing it to the bank. 'This is for killin' our pard, Ratsnake,' he snarled, swinging a great balled fist out at Will.

Will ducked and it grazed his temple. Then he quickly laid two sharp, hurting punches to Gordo's midriff. 'And that's for being so stupid,' he grated, now cursing under his breath for the want of being in some other place.

Gordo rolled his eyes with anticipation. 'You're makin' a mistake, Mister Pretty.'

71

Hardly a muscle moved in Will's face. He lashed out again with his right fist, and Gordo's head went back like a sprung hinge. The man's lips were splitting tight against his quid-stained teeth, and when his backside and heels hit the ground flat out, Will was on him.

But Gordo had an instinct for survival. He half turned, flung an arm around Will's neck, and clung tight. Will's knuckles drove into the back of his greasy head, but he swung himself over. Face down he rose to get on to all fours, with brute strength, reaching for another neck grip.

Will dodged him and threw all his weight forward. Gordo collapsed into the attack and together they rolled over and over through the bankside grass. They were both struggling for an advantage, ferociously clawing for each other.

They managed to climb to their feet, standing toe to toe, shocking each other with angry punches. Blood was pouring from their mouths and noses as Gordo snapped them into a clinch. They staggered from side to side, backwards and forwards before going down heavily, with Will underneath. Gordo thrust his left forearm under Will's chin and with the fingers of his right hand gouged at his eyes. Will lifted a leg as high as he could with his heel against Gordo. He kicked inward and thrust his boot back down sharply. With a bellow of pain Gordo flung himself away, staggering to regain his balance. One leg of his skin trousers had been ripped open, and blood streamed from where Will's spur had torn its way through.

They quartered the ground as they fought, throwing punches, manoeuvring for a handhold. Their lungs began to labour and rasp, and they staggered in unbalanced circles. The muscles in their arms were losing control, and their legs dragged heavily.

Gordo had the brute strength, but he lacked the thoughtful purpose of Will. Watching cautiously, Will knew that if the fight went on much longer, they'd both go down.

Gordo was slumping now, hardly able to lift his fists. He fought in defensive spurts, lowering his head, going forward in a despairing attack. A lucky aimless blow flung Will across the bole of a bankside oak, and, thrashing even more wildly, Gordo plunged forward to try and finish the fight.

But Will was still thinking, and he ducked, twisting quickly to one side. Gordo missed with his punch and rolled hard around the meat of the tree. Will grunted, eased himself back and settled for grabbing as much of Gordo's long hair and ears as he could. He drew the man's head back and smashed his face just once solidly against the ridges of crusty bark.

Gordo's body gave out and he sank to the ground, his head falling to the shallow water that curled close around the roots of the oak. Breathless,

Will lost his balance, and he fell exhausted on top of Gordo. For a short time, both men lay without stirring, then, nearly gagging at the beastly stench of Gordo's body, Will pushed himself away. But he stopped when he noticed the man's shattered face was under the water, being crushed against the bed pebbles. He gripped the leather jacket around the man's shoulders and, exerting his remaining strength, dragged the man's upper body clear of the water.

Taking support from the tree, Will looked down at the bruised face of the man he'd been fighting with. But he was too weary for sentiment, and, regaining his footing, he wiped his face with his wet hands. He climbed back up the low, sloping bank, raised his eyes to look back at the other three. 'I hope none of you fellers want to take it further,' he said quietly.

The riders sat still for a moment, then, with a new respect showing in their weather-worn faces, they walked their mounts through the shallows towards the unmoving Gordo.

'Next time, I won't be handing my gun in,' Will called out. Then he collected his belt from Laurel. Gathering the reins he swung up into the saddle, then immediately heeled his horse into motion.

As he loped up the slight incline, he heard Laurel's bay mare running after him. She caught up and rode alongside.

'That's got the introductions over, then? Do you know what I was thinking back there at the creek?'

'Yeah, the same as me. Was it the men I'd come looking for?'

They rode all the way into town in silence; only when they reached the livery stables did Laurel speak again.

'I'm surprised you can climb in and out of the saddle. You must hurt.'

'I do. I'm having an out-of-body experience. Your ma would probably have understood. No offence,' he added with a tired smile.

The hostler came out and took their horses. Will started to walk away, and again Laurel went after him.

'Why don't you go on home, Laurel?' This time he stopped, turned almost testily. 'I'm a manhunter, remember . . . a man-killer. And you're the sheriff's daughter. The two *ain't* favourable.'

Laurel reached out and touched his arm, then stepped back. 'You're a cattleman . . . a ranch owner. Do *you* remember, Will? And yes, I am the sheriff's daughter, but if anything happened to *him*, and if I was as pig-headed as you, I'd probably be doing the same.' Then she turned and walked hurriedly and huffily along to her house.

For a long moment, Will stared blankly into the distance, then he headed for the Rugosa Saloon. He didn't have much in the way of company, except a vengeance that gnawed at his vitals. But now, he realized, there was the possibility of breaking away.

.

11

'And that's the whole story, Pa, just as he told me,' Laurel said to her father, who was propped up in bed with the support of pillows. 'So he's no ordinary gunman as you'd have him. I guess over the past two years, he's had to fight to stay alive.'

'Only 'cause o' the trail he's chose. His foreman spent months teachin' him how to use a gun. Sorry, Laurel, but I don't hear too many extenuatin' circumstances there.' Wale rested a thoughtful gaze on his daughter. 'I don't suppose he told you who these killers are?'

'No. But he knows their names and what they look like.'

'An' he gave that big ox Gordo Krate a beatin'?' he asked with more favourable interest.

'Well, they were both beat up. He was the one able to walk away.'

'Hmm. One more thing, young lady. How come

he was so talkative with you, when we can hardly get a murmur out of him?'

Laurel lifted a tress of her long black hair to behind her shoulder. 'That's for him to say.'

'You fallen for him, daughter?'

'Why do you say that?' she asked, moving to the door.

'I dunno. I think you've already given me the answer.'

When Laurel returned with a tray, she was also bearing a light frown. 'I just remembered something,' she said. 'He's got the initials C.J. burnt into the back of his holster.'

Wade shifted against his pillows. 'C.J.? Maybe he ain't William Sparrow, after all.'

'Well, he doesn't strike me as a man who'd lie about his name, Pa. Here, you eat this.'

For a moment, Wale thought about asking for one of his deputies to look through the wanted dodgers. Instead, he looked down at the steaming bowl on the tray in his lap. 'What's this?' he asked. 'Your mother was the same, always comin' up with some awful posole mixture, when I was a tad off colour.'

Laurel watched silently for a while, as her father ate. Then she replied with, 'Can I ask him here for dinner tonight?'

'Hah. So you can shovel this hog mash down his neck? I wouldn't wish that on anyone.'

'So, can I?'

'Yeah, I suppose so. But take my advice, daughter, an' don't get too sweet on him. He's a loner if ever I seen one. He'll likely disappear as soon as his work's done.'

Laurel leaned forward and kissed her father on the forehead. 'If you know so much about him, you won't be askin' uncomfortable questions.'

'Let me put it another way, Laurel. If any man should do you harm, there ain't a hole anywhere on God's earth deep enough for him to hide in. Now, ask him to call in and pay his respects when he arrives.'

'I will if you promise to rest between now and then.'

'Aah, don't fuss. So what's for dinner? An' don't tell me you were waitin' for me to say it's OK.'

'Steak pie, baked potatoes, mixed vegetables, fresh-baked bread for the sopping, canned peaches, cream and strong coffee.' She took his tray and went to the door. 'If you behave, I might leave this door ajar so you can see us. Go to sleep.'

Down at the jailhouse, Cooter Lennon was pacing back and forth in front of the desk, with a nervous expression on his face. He glanced at Juno Hemsby, who was working on some papers, then he walked to the far end of the office and sat down. He tapped his foot to a tune that had been trapped in his head ever since the dance. He whistled, stopped, looked at Hemsby again, then stood up and paced the floor. After another couple minutes, he stepped to the door, poked his head out and looked up and down the street.

Hemsby looked up and smiled tolerantly. 'OK, Cooter, you got my attention. Come back in an' tell me what's buggin' you,' he said.

'I can't. How do I sit still when Elodie's comin' by?' young Lennon spluttered.

'Easy. Just trip or somethin' the next time you pass a goddamn chair.'

'You think it's funny, don't you? It's a big step I'm takin', Juno. This is serious . . . dead serious.'

'So's makin' coffee,' the older deputy drawled.

'Elodie's goin' to stop by here any minute an' say whether or not she's goin' to marry me, an' all you can think about is *coffee*?' Lennon almost yelled.

'Yeah, that's about it, Cooter. I can't believe you actually got round to askin' that sweet, pretty little thing to spend the rest of her natural with you. Even if you did, she's not goin' to give you a reply while I'm sittin' here.'

'Why do you say that, Juno? What's wrong with me?'

'Nothing, Cooter,' Laurel Wale interjected as she came through the door. 'Is he making fun of you again?'

'Yes, ma'am, as usual. An' now I've got office

chores,' Lennon said and excused himself, making his way back through to the cell block.

'Hello, Laurel. What can I do for you?' Hemsby relaxed, started to build himself a smoke.

'Do you think you could find Will Sparrow, and tell him I'd like to see him?'

'I can take you straight to him,' Hemsby said as he stood up. 'He went into the Rugosa an hour ago. By the look on his face when he went in, I'd say he's still there.'

On the boardwalk he took Laurel by the arm and led her across the increasingly busy street. He asked her to take a seat outside the saloon, saying he wouldn't be a moment.

Once through the swing doors Hemsby stopped dead in his tracks. To the right, and from where he'd been sitting, Will Sparrow was walking slowly towards the bar, his eyes fixed on the figure of Manuel Pinto.

The Mexican hired gun was grinning at him casually, leaning an elbow on the bartop. Not another man in the room moved, but every eye was on the two men.

Hemsby took a good long look at Pinto. *I told him he was as good as dead. Looks like it could be now,* he thought to himself, seeing Pinto's grin beginning to fade.

'*Buen día,* William Sparrow,' Pinto said tightly. 'You come to buy my whiskey?'

'Yeah, the prize for missing me last night. I know it was you, Manuel,' Will answered. 'When I rode out of Alcalde, I had you down as a common border chilli. You *and* your brother. But shooting at me from the dark takes a certain kind of cowardly scum.' Will's voice trailed off as he drilled his grey eyes into Pinto. 'You could have hit the girl I was talking to. She's not much more than a kid.'

'And Felipe was my *brother*,' Pinto said, straightening from the bar. 'You moved when I fired. That makes me sad . . . *muy triste.*'

'Well, you leave *me* no alternative,' Will responded, his right fist piling up between them to crack under Pinto's dark jaw, '*and* a tad angered.'

Pinto went reeling, clawing for the bar with one hand to steady himself. Will followed up quickly, sinking his fist into Pinto's stomach, doubling him up. Will then drove his fist upwards, sending Pinto to his knees. He stood back, waiting as Pinto got back to his feet with blood oozing slowly from his bitten tongue. Pinto spat a Spanish oath, then reached out and grabbed the back of a chair, hurling it at Will, who ducked. But Will wasn't quick enough and went crashing back heavily against the bar.

Pinto smirked, moving in fast with two good blows to Will's face. Will grunted, lashed out and clipped Pinto above the left eye. Pinto swore as Will pounded a powerful right across his mouth, breaking teeth. Will split his own knuckle skin, but as

82

Pinto stumbled, he pushed away from the bar, smashing his fist again into the side of the Mexican's face.

With rasping breaths, both men circled each other. Pinto lunged, pulling Will to the floor, thumping a fist into his ribs as they fell. Will's breath whooshed from his lungs, as Pinto groped at his throat.

Will's head started to spin. He felt dizzy, and still Pinto squeezed and pressed. Will knew he had to break his hold, or die face up on the dirty pun- cheoned boards. He reached a hand up around the back of Pinto's head, in one swift movement took a handful of hair and jerked the man's head back. With his other hand, he jabbed hard into the middle of Pinto's stretched throat. As the man released his grip, Will rolled to one side and Pinto fell away.

Will struggled to his feet, his head still muzzy. Pinto looked at him, and, in dogged challenge, he too made it back up. But Will waited only a moment before driving his left fist deep into Pinto's belly. With virtually all his muscle spent, he then threw a right that landed with brutal impact against Pinto's temple. Pinto hurtled sideways to crash into a table. For a second, he lay across the surface of beery wood as though paralyzed, then his arms and head dropped and he collapsed to the floor.

Will cursed from the pain that shot up his arm from his damaged finger bones. 'If she was that kind of girl, I'm sure Miss Wale would have appreciated that,' he grated.

'When you've finished here, there's a young lady outside to see you, Sparrow. Don't keep her waitin' like you do everyone else,' Hemsby called, as he pounded testily across the room.

Wiping Pinto's blood from his face, Will turned and gave the deputy an impassive look. Then, sucking his raw knuckles, he went and pushed at the swing doors, avoiding the eyes of Cato, who was standing dumbfounded behind the bar.

12

Will stepped out on to the boardwalk. He took a deep breath, offering a relieved smile when he saw it was Laurel waiting for him.

'I heard most of that . . . saw some of it. Difficult not to. I had a quick look over the doors,' she said haltingly and with obvious concern.

Will looked but said nothing. At the present, most of his feelings carried little sensation.

'That was the man who shot at us last night, wasn't it?' Laurel continued.

'Me. It was me he shot at, not you, Laurel.' Will was going to ask why she wanted to see him, when his attention was drawn to the horse and buggy coming from the western end of the main street. He stood watchful and unmoving as the vehicle drew to a stop in front of the saloon porch.

The driver was a striking middle-aged woman with salt-and-pepper hair and grey eyes. She wore a high-priced set of range clothes, sitting cool and composed as she ignored Laurel and estimated Will.

'Hello, Will,' she said. 'You've grown some. And been in a fight, by the look of it.'

Will felt a chilliness run the length of his body. 'Yeah. Most boys do both in ten years or more.'

'Still holding on to that hate? It can eat you up, you know?' she said, silently flinching under Will's coldness. 'You just don't know. Your feelings are born from the fact that me and your pa were as suited as chiggers and toes. Is that why you hated me, Will?'

Will walked to the edge of the porch and looked directly at her. 'It seems you were late on support through thick an' thin, maybe took off a little too soon,' he said callously. 'Wolf Run is now one of the finest ranches in the San Louis Valley.'

'I'm doing all right. I don't want for anything.'

'Yeah, except for a heart an' soul.'

'You think people don't get things wrong, shouldn't be forgiven? I'm still your mother, Will.'

'You haven't been that since the day I was born. Probably before,' Will snapped harshly. For the first time in years, he could feel his temperament slipping.

Laurel touched his arm gently, and he jumped as if stung. 'Christ, I wish people wouldn't keep doing that. I'm not some sort of family pet.'

'I'm sorry,' Laurel blurted out. 'Please walk me home. I'm beginning to not like it here.'

'Well, right now, this isn't the place I'd choose to be, Laurel. But I've got twenty years of bile on this woman.'

'I don't think that's what she came into town for. Come on, let's go.' This time Laurel pulled him away, led him by the arm along the boardwalk. Will accompanied her woodenly, his fists clenched and his teeth grinding.

From the buggy, the woman gestured with her whip. 'Stay away from him, Laurel,' she called out. 'He was born before I married his father. Seems pretty apt to me.'

Will wrenched his arm free of Laurel and turned, his anger at last getting the better of him. He took only a couple of steps, though, then stopped. Two rifles and three guns were pointed right at his chest.

'Hold on there, young 'un,' one man said. 'Alma Oldring's been in these parts for a long time now, an' us folk here have come to like her a powerful lot; enough to pull a gun on them who wish her harm.'

'An' you've been here three days an' already killed two men. We don't like it, mister . . . you an' your kind,' another joined in.

'Well, that's just fine, you miserable sons-of-bitches, because I'll make it half a dozen dead men, if you don't point those guns somewhere else,' Will threatened dangerously.

A murmur went through a gathering crowd, heads nodding and arms waving animatedly. But Will was staring back at his mother, his face showing signs of confusion and uncertainty, being taken unawares.

'Please, Will,' Laurel persisted. 'Listen to me . . . my side of the story.'

Will took no notice because three riders were fast approaching along the street. When they drew to a halt alongside and in front of the buggy, Will recognized one of them as the rancher he'd been told was Cyrus Oldring. But now his recollection had the man nailed as a one-time top hand from Wolf Run.

Oldring dismounted stiffly, then stepped up to the buggy. 'Alma. You leave the ranch without saying anything. What's up?'

Alma pointed at Will. 'Hello, Cyrus, aren't you going to say hello? You remember Will, don't you?'

Oldring's eyebrows arched. 'William Sparrow? Young Will Sparrow?'

'There was only the one,' Alma assured him with a thin smile.

Oldring ran sweating palms down the legs of his dark trousers. He'd seen Will side with the sheriff at the dance the night before, but he hadn't recognized him.

'All of you, put those guns away,' he ordered the few men who were still toying with their pistols and rifles.

'Better still, move on.' Juno Hemsby's voice boomed in accord. 'I see another man with a gun out of its holster today, I'll lock him up for a month, goddamnit.'

Oldring brushed past a few disgruntled onlookers until he was close to Will. 'Hello, Will. How long has it been?' he greeted.

'Must be twelve years, give or take.'

'In life, there's some things you can't see coming, Will. It's little compensation I guess, but I never had anything against your pa. In many ways, I admired him.'

'Yeah, and his wife,' Will replied bitterly.

'She stopped loving him. You can't blame her for that, or me. There's no defence against what happened. Neither of us set out that way.'

'You could have pulled out any time you liked. You both chose to make some dirt and then rub Pa's nose in it. So to hell with your pardons, mister.'

A towner swore at Will's irate words and swung up his rifle. But Will was alert to the impulsive movement; in the blink of an eye, his hand levelled the barrel of his Navy Colt directly between the man's eyes. However, he didn't have to think about pulling the trigger. Juno Hemsby had also been expecting such a move, and like Will, had reacted instantly. His big Dragoon's Colt stove in the crown of the man's range hat, denting the man's head, dropping him like a sack of potatoes in the middle of the boardwalk.

Hemsby looked down at the unconscious man, lifting his Colt to fire twice into the air. His eyes met Will's and he saw the look of silent thanks.

Moments later, the crowd was breaking up as Cooter Lennon ran through them, glancing at Will and Laurel, to stop beside Hemsby.

'Two shots, Juno. What's the trouble?' he asked, breathless.

Hemsby pointed to the man lying on the board-walk. 'Take him to the jailhouse an' lock him up.' He then said to the few who were still hanging around, 'Remember what I said about your gunplay. If you've somethin' to say, just say it.' Then he puffed out his cheeks and leaned back against the clinkered wall of the saloon.

Laurel stepped to Will's side. 'It's over. Take me home,' she said.

'In a minute,' he replied, once more looking to face his mother. 'Just tell me one thing,' he asked. 'Am I William Sparrow's son?'

Alma Oldring gave a curious, triumphant smile. 'Oh yes, you're your father's son all right, Will. But there's more of me in you, than of him.'

'How the hell would you know?' Will returned sharply as he turned away.

As they walked, Laurel could feel Will trembling. But the sun was beating down now, and she knew it wasn't from cold or fear. She slid her hand down his arm and linked her fingers through his, her dark eyes searching for an expression on his face.

'If it's not one thing it's another, eh, Will?' she said in a weak attempt at lifting the moment. 'Didn't you have any idea where your mother was? What had happened to her?'

'Now and again, I suppose. Not five minutes ago I didn't.'

Laurel lowered her head. 'I can't imagine what that's like.'

'Why's it so important for me to walk you home?' he asked, when they arrived at the Wales' front gate. 'You do pretty well on your own, I seem to remember.'

Laurel smiled. 'I was going to ask you to have dinner with me tonight, and I didn't want the rest of the town to know it. You might have turned me down.'

'No, I wouldn't do that. But I doubt your father would appreciate me eating at his table. Have you run it by him?'

'Yes, and he wants to exchange compliments when you arrive.'

'Hah, more likely exchange a few practised threats. Thank you, Laurel. I'll look forward to it.'

'If you can stay out of trouble that long, say seven?'

'Yeah, seven's fine.'

Laurel was so pleased she stretched up, quickly brushing her lips against the stubble of Will's lower cheek. Then without another word she turned and walked calmly towards her front door.

Will narrowed his eyes, stared blankly at the front door for a few moments after it had closed. Then he stepped out on to the street, jolting back when a buckboard rumbled by as if the driver hadn't seen him. He looked down at his clothes, seeing the dust and dirt, the torn shoulder of his shirt, the worn knees of his Levis, the scuffed boots.

A few minutes later he stepped into the dimness of Baxter's Mercantile and crossed over to the counter. Mose Baxter was a friendly, easy-going man, who hoped one day to marry Elodie Wesker's widowed mother. Presently, he was serving a lady customer who, on seeing Will, gave a nervous look and decided to come back later.

Baxter smiled tolerantly at Will and asked how he could help.

'I'd like one of those linen shirts,' he said, pointing at the shelf behind Baxter. 'A new pair of trousers and the best boots you've got in store – black and shiny. I'll be paying cash money, if you're wondering.'

Baxter wrapped the clothing, took Will's dollars and thanked him for his custom.

13

A few minutes after seven that night, Laurel went to the front door of her home. She was convinced that in the silence after the knock, Will would hear the thumping of her heart, even if he couldn't see it through her dress. She licked her lips, rolling her bracelet around her wrist for the umpteenth time before opening the door.

Her considered greeting of, 'Good evening, please come in and make yourself at home,' came out as, 'Hello, Will, I'm glad you came.'

Will entered and stood just inside, waiting for Laurel to close the door.

Laurel took his hat and placed it on the chest of drawers in a corner of the parlour. 'I guess a new outfit didn't include a hat,' she said with a smile.

'Replacing a hat's a much more serious thing,' Will replied, admiring the long, doeskin dress that Laurel had decided to wear.

'I'll take whatever you're thinking as a compliment,' she said, acknowledging Will's appraising look. 'Would you like to sit in the easy chair – have a drink, maybe? Dinner won't be long.'

Laurel poured a generous whiskey, handed it to him and sat close by at the corner of an armless chair. 'There's something I meant to ask you,' she said. 'The initials on your holster. They're not yours, are they?'

'No. It's for Copperhead Joad.'

'Who was he?'

'One of a bunch of fellers. They made themselves a name along the Nueces Strip.'

'So how did you come by it?'

'I didn't kill him for the rig, if that's what you're thinking. He's my ranch foreman, only now his name is *Rufus* Joad,' Will said, taking a sip of the whiskey. 'About ten years ago he was bushwhacked – shot in the back by an army deserter. Everyone thought him dead, but he wasn't. My pa found him, tended his wounds and brought him home. For reasons that weren't too far from obvious, he gave him the name of Rufus and the offer of a new life. He must have seen something in him, I guess. Anyway, Rufus has been with us ever since, which kind of proves it. I bought the gun from him. It was made in London, England, and I paid him top dollar.'

Laurel nodded understandingly. 'Having seen it,

I had to ask. I could have got to imagining all sorts of things. Would you like to go in and talk to Pa now, while I go and set the table?'

Will stood up. 'Was that part of the deal? If you let me, I can put a knife and fork around a plate.'

'No. You go in and see him. He's obviously got something to say.' Laurel nodded at a closed door. 'Go on. He's not armed.'

Will moved reluctantly to the door. He gave Laurel a questioning look over his shoulder, then swung the door open. The sheriff was propped up on his bed, and in the glow of a wall lantern Will could see the man's tired, drawn face. He closed the door quietly, crossed over to stand at the foot of the bed.

'You're looking better than the last time I saw you,' he said.

'An' you're a dadburn liar,' Wale growled. 'That's the doc an' his wife, my two deputies, my own daughter, an' now you, all sayin' how well I look. I must look like I'm at death's door.'

'Laurel tells me you've been hurt worse.'

'Yeah, when I was thirty-two, not *fifty*-two, god-damnit.' Wale gave Will a thoughtful, calculating look. 'Juno Hemsby gave me an account of what happened today.'

'I figured he would.'

'Is Alma Oldring really your mother?'

'Yeah. We never had an issue with that,' Will said

flatly. 'Do you know her well?'

'Well enough. She came here about ten years ago with Cyrus Oldring. For the first few months she got attention from Farley Rochester. Huh, sometimes I thought Farley was goin' to fight Cyrus in the street, he was so bothered.'

'That's the sort of yarn I could be less interested in.'

Wale gave Will an unmoved look and continued. 'Alma got their commitment sorted eventually – has done fine ever since. She's well liked here in Magdalena, so don't hold it against folk for gettin' snuffy.'

'I don't. It's a hayshaker's trigger finger that worries me,' Will said with a slight headshake.

'Juno also told me about the fight between you an' Manuel Pinto. He said he didn't know what it was about, but I think he did.'

Will gave a look of understanding of the sheriff's guile. 'You must have heard the gunshots.'

'Yeah, it would've woke me if I'd been dead, for Chris'sakes.'

'It was Manuel trying to get even with me for killing Felipe.'

'You figure he'll try it again?'

'I doubt it, but I don't know. I did kill his brother. But if he does, it won't be anywhere near here. That I promise.'

'Uh-huh. Laurel told me why you're here in

Magdalena, Will Sparrow. An' before you get to thinkin' she's spoken out of turn, remember I'm her father.'

'Are you going to do anything about it?'

'That depends on how you aim to kill 'em. The two men you're after.'

'They'll be facing me, Sheriff, I can tell you that much. And they'll have more of a chance than they gave my pa.'

Wale shut his eyes for a moment, then squinted down at his gnarled hands. 'Just make sure you kill 'em legal, son. Any other way an' you'll be answerin' to my badge.'

Will was saved from a response when Laurel called his name. He opened the door for her and she came in carrying a tray of warm sourdough rolls, cheese and coffee. She placed it on her father's lap, then stood back smiling.

'We're leaving you now, so's you can dunk the bread,' she said playfully. 'If there's any pie left over, I'll bring it to you later.'

Will followed Laurel from the room, amused, if not a little envious, at the way Laurel sparred with her father.

'You must come over for dinner more often,' Wale called out, dropping all his gruff authority. 'It's been weeks ... months since I been fed like this.'

In the kitchen, Laurel sat opposite Will. Even

though she knew he must be hungry, she noticed he ate slowly, savouring every mouthful.

'You've got your mother's hair colour,' she said when their eyes met.

'It doesn't mean much. My pa was that colour too,' Will replied, and went on to finish his meal in silence. He pushed his plate to one side and leaned back. 'That was some meal. Best I've put away in many a moon,' he complimented.

'A few more slices of peach, then?'

'I couldn't. That's a physical fact, and not for the want of trying.'

'OK. I'll save it for Pa. Shall we have coffee out back? It's a cool evening . . . shouldn't be anything much biting.'

'I'd like that,' Will said, standing up. He pushed his chair in close to the table and carried the two cups out through the back door, waiting while Laurel sat down in one of the cane chairs before sitting himself.

'I got a bit snuffy today out there in the street,' he said quietly, but with clear, pent-up feeling.

'Yes, you did. But how many of us bump into our mothers after not seeing them for ten years? It's an understandable response.'

'Yeah, I guess.'

Laurel turned side-on in her seat to face him. 'Have you *forgot* my name, Will? Or are you too discomfited with the familiarity?'

'No, Laurel, I'm sorry. I like your name. I'm just out of the habit, I guess,' he smiled tiredly. 'Tell me,' he said, changing the subject. 'How big is that Circle O of Cyrus Oldring's?'

'Big. It's on the same scale as the Rochester spread, and that's saying something.'

'Is it really doing well?'

'Very well, I believe. They certainly live off the best of everything.'

'Hmm. And you've lived here all your life?'

'Yes, born and bred. I went to the hill school, just out of town. My mother died of consumption when I was twelve, and I've been taking care of Pa since.'

'Haven't you got a young man . . . an admirer? There must be someone.'

Laurel shook her head. 'No. Well, there's always been *someone*, but no one of any significance.' She leaned over in her chair. 'I think maybe it's Pa. Him and his office, that has them running scared. Still, how about you, Will? I'm not likely to forget what you said, but are you sure there isn't a girl waiting on your return?'

'I'm sure, Laurel. And I said what I said, because of it. I'm not a double-dealer.'

Laurel stood up then and moved over to stand in front of him. She reached down and took one of his hands then pulled him to his feet. 'When I saw you for the first time, standing at the door with Juno Hemsby, something happened,' she began. 'And today, out at the creek I felt the same thing. You're not alone with those thoughts and feelings, Will.'

Will squeezed Laurel's hand, held it up close to his chest. 'But you probably will be. You must know I'll be riding on,' he answered.

'Do I, Will? I remember you saying you weren't in such a hurry any more.'

'I wasn't. I'm not. But either way, you don't want to live on an uncertainty, Laurel. I reckon your pa would say the same thing, if he saw us like this. He'd find the strength to kick me back to where I come from.'

Then, as if on a timely cue, they both started, stepping hastily apart.

'A'hem,' Cooter Lennon coughed out from the back door. 'Evenin', folks. Sorry to disturb you an' all, but Sheriff reckoned you'd be here,' the deputy said, stepping closer. 'He called me in when I knocked,' he added, a touch diffidently.

'That's all right, Cooter. What is it?' Laurel asked.

'I came to tell you the good news,' he said, beaming from ear to ear.

'What good news, Cooter?'

'Me an' Elodie are gettin' married Friday. I thought you'd be interested – want to know.'

'Of course, Cooter,' Laurel exclaimed happily. 'I'm glad and pleased for you both.' She stepped up and kissed him on the cheek.

'Yeah, congratulations, Deputy,' Will said quietly.

'I guess there's some will have to find something else to rib you about.'

'I guess. Thank you, Will. I did mean to talk to you about Felipe Pinto. You beat me to the shooting.'

'Sorry about that, Cooter, but it's not some sort of contest, you know. Besides, this isn't the time.'

'No, maybe not. Well you an' Laurel are invited to the weddin',' he said cheerily.

'Look forward to it, if I'm around,' Will told him as he headed for the door.

Laurel and the young deputy followed on to the parlour, watching silently as Will picked up his hat.

'The finest fixings in town, Laurel. The sort that stays in the mind for a while. A very goodnight to you,' Will said, slipping out and closing the door after him.

Cooter dropped his arms to his sides. 'He's a strange one,' he said.

'He is that, Cooter,' Laurel replied, almost absent-mindedly. 'But I think there's a lot that's making him so.'

'Yeah. Well, goodnight, Miss Laurel.' With that, Lennon left the Wales' home.

At the same time, in a large house on the western outskirts of town, Addison Rugosa was pacing around the floor of his step-down den. He was gulping whiskey in between looking daggers at

Manuel Pinto.

'What the hell were you trying to do, Mano? Killing Sparrow's only going to bring a brace of lawmen snapping at our heels. Except you didn't kill him.'

'Felipe was my brother,' Pinto said sourly. 'What do you expect?'

'You were lucky.' Rugosa flicked a telling glance at Pinto's cut and bruised face.

Pinto fingered his sore throat, the lump on his temple. One eye was already puffed and swollen. 'He's made too many mistakes. I'll get him,' he promised.

'Not until we finish the job, you won't,' the saloon owner said. 'And we'll need another two good men, now that Felipe and Venters aren't with us. I'm reluctant to ask, but have you got an idea on that?'

Pinto crossed over to a long side-table and reached for the whiskey decanter. He poured himself a generous measure, and immediately drained the glass. 'I can find them,' he asserted.

Rugosa gave him a foxy look. 'Like who?'

Pinto grinned coldly as he poured another whiskey. 'Toll Judkins and Oliver Patch.'

Rugosa looked surprised. 'They work for Oldring.'

'Yeah. Patch is ramrod.'

'Why them in particular?'

'Two years ago they shot Will Sparrow's old man.'

Rugosa cursed with surprise. 'You're sure? You're sure it's them?'

'Sparrow's hunted them down. That's why he's here. I knew it when me and Felipe saw him in your bar.'

Rugosa cursed again. He swirled the whiskey in his glass, then stood up, stepped to the front window and looked into the darkness. 'We take the bank and its payroll money on Friday.'

'That's too soon.'

'Talk in the saloon's on young Cooter Lennon getting hitched on Friday. That means most of the town will be in and around the church. So, "too soon" don't figure. It's our only chance.'

'*Bueno*. You give me the plan and I ride to see Patch and Judkins.'

Rugosa turned away from the window. 'Pour yourself another drink and sit down. I'll give you the setup,' he said with a calculating smile.

14

The next morning Will rolled from his hotel bed. He was still feeling tired after spending a restless night with thoughts of Laurel Wale. She had really disturbed and moved him.

A little later he entered the Beef 'n' Biscuit and sat at the counter. He nodded to Elodie Wesker when she smiled at him. 'Just coffee this morning, Elodie. Strong. No cream, no sweetening.'

'Is Alma Oldring really your mother? It's all around town,' Elodie said, placing his coffee in front of him.

'It must be right, then,' he answered after taking a sip.

'Me and Cooter's getting married tomorrow.'

'I know, Elodie. That too's all around town,' Will said, and smiled. 'I got an invitation from the lucky groom himself.'

'Laurel's agreed to be bridesmaid, and Mr Baxter

is giving me away.'

'Fine. They're all lucky folk, Elodie. You must be thrilled.'

Will finished his coffee, and took his leave. Beneath the overhang of the Rugosa Saloon he sat down, tilting the deckchair back against the wall. A full hour later when Cato opened up, he moved inside, picked up a copy of the *Albuquerque Tribune* from the bar and sat at his usual table.

Further along the main street, in front of the jail-house, Cooter Lennon and Juno Hemsby were watching the stranger who rode slowly towards them.

'Who the hell's this?' Lennon said with guarded movement of his lips.

'Dunno. Looks like a tough little *hombre*, though,' Hemsby replied.

The man pulled in, swung down and tied his weary gelding to the hitchrail. He was of lean build and his hair was steel grey. His clothes gave the appearance of someone who had travelled a long distance, and Hemsby noted the short-barrelled carbine that was holstered alongside the saddle.

The man stepped up to the deputies, gave Lennon a quick glance and then looked directly at Hemsby. 'I'm looking for a man named William Sparrow – Will Sparrow.' The man's voice was even, no louder than it need be.

Hemsby stiffened visibly. 'What's your business with him?'

'Outside o' the sheriff's office, that's a likely request,' the older man conceded. 'Perhaps I should have asked plainer. Do you know of William Sparrow? If so, where can I likely find him?' He saw the unease, the question in the deputies' eyes. 'I'm Rufus Joad,' he added.

'Sparrow's ramrod?' Hemsby suggested.

'Yes, if that's what he's told you.'

Hemsby knew he was looking at a one-time, dangerous and near legendary border gunman. Yet by the size of him, you could imagine a puff of wind destroying him. His face was weather-beaten, devoid of emotion, but his eyes were ever lively.

'He's booked into the Spanish Peaks Hotel, eats at the Beef 'n' Biscuit, and drinks at the Rugosa Saloon. That's probably where his is now, and all your money buys, Mr Joad,' Hemsby told him.

Joad smiled, turned slightly and scanned the street. 'Hope no harm's come to the boy,' he said, almost sounding like a threat. Then he stepped down from the boardwalk and headed straight for the saloon.

'He's even got the same goddamn walk,' Hemsby said, watching as Rufus Joad sauntered off. 'There's layers o' hard bark there, Cooter,' he added thoughtfully.

Joad pushed the batwings open and entered, stepping to one side. He saw the handful of early customers and Cato the barkeep, then the loner sitting over by the far wall watching him. He moved unhurriedly to the bar, bought himself a beer and went to Will's table.

'You're a hard man to find,' he said.

'Good,' Will replied. He eased his chair back, and stood up, leaving his hands flat on the table. 'What are you doing here, Rufus? You're supposed to be taking care of the ranch.'

'I'm here because I haven't heard a peep from you in nearly six months. How was I supposed to know you're alive and kicking? Jake and Dutch are taking care of the ranch.'

'I'd be one hell of a lot happier knowing *you* were back there,' Will said, his grey eyes telling Joad he wasn't pleased.

'The ranch is in good hands, Will.'

'Goddamnit, Rufus, I don't care how good they are. I'm saying, I don't need you *here*,' Will rasped.

Joad followed Will over to the bar, stood beside him with a wry grin on his face. 'Say you're glad to see me. Admit it, you're overjoyed that I'm here,' he ribbed, as Will ordered two whiskeys.

'On the house,' Cato said. 'Any friend o' yours is a friend of ours.'

Will shook his head and snapped some coins on to the counter, then he swung his eyes to Joad's lined, weathered face. He broke into a slow smile and the men gripped hands.

'I suppose you've got to be somewhere,' Will said.

'But you really weren't meant to find me. How'd you do it?'

'Sheriff in Dixon Valedo told me of a feller with yellow hair who shot and killed a man. He said it was a fair fight, that he thought you rode south.'

Will saw the questioning look in Joad's eyes. 'His name was Lou Grissom. He used to be a corporal.'

Joad nodded slowly. 'And the others?'

'Grissom told me they were here or hereabouts.' Will took a sip of whiskey. 'So what are your plans now you've found me?'

'Same as yours, I guess.'

'No, Rufus. I would like you to rest up a spell, then ride back to the ranch.'

'I'm not going anywhere without you, Will. Get that into your thick head. Both Jake and Dutch are on a *do well* bonus. The other hands take their orders, just as they would from you and me.'

Will squinted at the whiskey glass while he considered for a moment. 'Two years is a long time gone,' he said. 'How's the place shaping up?'

'Just fine. We could use a hands-on boss now and again, though.'

'Won't be long, Rufus. We'll ride back together.'

Joad toyed with his glass. 'We bought a new bull. A big, pedigree Hereford,' he said suddenly, breaking the heavy mood.

'I look forward to meeting him. Alma's in Magdalena.'

'What?'

'My mother, Alma. She's here in Magdalena.'

Joad snapped his head up. He stared at Will's face for a long time, then cursed low and long. 'How? When?'

Will had no time to answer before the batwings slammed open and Farley Rochester paced determinedly over to them.

'I'm Farley Rochester. Which one of you two's Sparrow?' he barked, his face already shaded with anger.

Will looked at him more with surprise and interest than anxiety. 'That's me. Why?'

'You shot dead Polk Chatham, then rode on to my land and beat up Gordo Krate. He's laid up with a nose spread half across his face. Who the hell are you?'

'Chatham called the fight, called me into the street. As for your cowboy, he wanted my hide for doing it. I obliged him.'

'You were on my land, and my men had the right to throw you off. That's what Gordo was doing, and on my say-so.'

'Wrong. I was leaving. That's when your man started the fight. He was speaking to my back. I thought it best to turn and fight rather than have him shoot into it.'

'That's not how I heard it.'

'Well, to coin an old phrase, it wouldn't be, would

it, Mr Rochester?'

Rochester reached out to grab Will by the shoulder, but found himself abruptly confronted by Rufus Joad.

'Best not to do that, mister. He's never liked being touched like that. I know him.' Joad smiled icily.

Two of Rochester's riders now pushed forward, half drawing their guns when they saw their boss being defied.

'No need for trouble, boys . . . anyone,' Will said. 'I don't want any truck with this man, and he doesn't want any with me.'

Rochester turned to Will. 'Stay away from my men,' he warned, then turned to Joad. 'You tell him,' he added.

The rancher gave a final, hostile glare at both men, then strode from the bar.

Joad looked at Will. He was about to say something, but Will cut him short.

'I don't need you, so I'm going to have to fire you,' Will said.

'You wouldn't fire me. My getting in the way's an advantage when trouble's got you in its sights.'

Joad followed Will out on to the boardwalk, stopping in his tracks when he saw Rose Rochester sitting proudly in the Dearborn rig.

'Good God, Will. No *wonder* you don't come home. I thought that kind of lady didn't venture west of the Mississippi,' he whispered, taking a step aside.

One of the hired hands helped Rochester's niece down, then with a flounce she walked over to Will.

'I'm Rose Rochester, and you're the man they're all talking about,' she declared, looking up at him. 'Tell me, Mr Sparrow, how did you make such a mess of Gordo Krate's face? Did you use your gun?'

'No, ma'am. I told his horse to kick him. Beast near jumped at the chance,' Will responded to the slight sarcasm.

Rose didn't smile. 'By the looks of things, I'd say he gave you some trouble too.'

'Yes, ma'am, he did, specially my knuckles. He hasn't got the softest of head bones.'

'You've incurred my uncle's wrath, haven't you?'

'Yeah, he's just been letting me know,' Will said, looking warily up and down the street.

'Don't you think he's got good reason?'

'*He* certainly thinks so,' Will muttered, looking distractedly over Rose's shoulder. 'I've got to . . . erm, please excuse me,' he said, stepping down from the boardwalk.

Laurel Wale was on the other side of the street. She was carrying a marketing bag, not turning away quick enough to disguise the miffed, irritated look.

She strode more briskly towards Baxter's, and Will caught up to her just as she was about to enter the store.

'Laurel, hold on a moment,' he said.

'Hello, Will,' Laurel replied with a quickly fashioned look of surprise. 'I would have said something, but I could see you were busy.'

'Well, that was then, this is now, and I want to talk to you – ask you something.'

'Can it wait a few minutes while I see Mr Baxter?'

'Yeah, I guess.'

Will waited for her to come out, then he followed on in the direction of her house. 'I was going to ask how your father was. But better still, are you a tad prickly about something?' he asked.

'I think maybe I am, yes.'

'Why? I already told you how I feel about you. That's not likely to change by me passing the time of day with Miss Rochester.'

'No, it's not, and I'm sorry, Will. I'm on edge with Pa . . . one thing and another. Who was that man you were with? I haven't seen him around.'

'That's Rufus Joad,' Will replied, taking a look back to the saloon where Joad was still talking to Rose Rochester. 'The C.J., remember? And it looks like Miss Rochester has found herself an admirer. It's a side of old Rufus I've never seen before.'

'Pa's always saying, there's many fine tunes still being played on old fiddles,' Laurel said, and handed Will a parcel. 'If the folk around here are going to chinwag, we might as well give them something to chinwag about,' she added with a mischievous smile, and slipped her free arm through his.

At the gate to her house, Laurel took back her parcel. 'I'd like to see you tonight, Will,' she said.

'Good, and that goes for me too. And I've remembered the other thing I wanted to ask you. Do you know a man called Patch? Oliver Patch? Heard his name, maybe?'

Laurel repeated the man's name, thinking for a moment. 'That's Cyrus Oldring's ramrod, I'm sure. I've only seen him in town a few times. Why?'

'Just wondered. Take your shopping in,' he said quietly. 'I'll see you later.'

Laurel nodded and watched him walk away. Then she turned and walked slowly but thoughtfully to her door.

Fifteen minutes later, Rufus Joad found Will at the livery stables. 'Are you going somewhere?' he asked, as Will saddled the buckskin mare.

'I've heard that Patch is ramrodding the Circle O, so what do you think?'

'You want me to come along, get in the way, maybe?'

'No, I don't,' Will replied in a low voice as he tugged at the cinch. He led the mare from the livery and swung into the saddle. 'If I don't come back, Wolf Run's all yours, Rufus. If there's someone who doesn't like it, shoot 'em. Either that, or present the affidavit that's lodged at the Monte Vista Bank. It's up to you.' Then Will gave the horse a nudge with his heels and headed west along the main street.

Joad looked on inscrutably. 'Drinks are on me when I see you,' he muttered softly to himself. Then he went back to give Juno Hemsby some competition with Rose Rochester.

15

One hour after leaving Magdalena, Will rode across the front yard of the Circle O Ranch. He reined in at the water trough, sitting quietly watching the front door of the ranch house while his mare took a long drink.

It wasn't long before the door opened and Alma Oldring stepped on to the broad veranda.

'I knew you'd come. If only out of idle curiosity,' she said, studying the impassive face of her son. 'Or is it to say goodbye?'

'Neither. I'm looking for your ramrod, Oliver Patch.'

'Oliver Patch? What do you want him for?' she asked, shivering slightly at the icy look in Will's eyes. 'He's away checking the boundaries. He took the line boss with him – probably won't be back before tomorrow night.'

'How far's that?'

'Six, maybe seven miles west.' Alma stepped to the handrail that fronted the property. 'It would take you a day and you could miss him.'

The buckskin raised a foreleg, pawed the ground and snorted. Will turned in his saddle, stared out at the western ridges.

'I asked what you wanted him for,' Alma cut in on his thoughts.

Will switched his gaze back to his mother. 'Two years ago, him and two others rode in and shot Pa dead . . . murdered him.' Will took off his hat, ran his hand across his corn-coloured hair. 'This line boss of yours,' he continued, 'has he got a moon-eye, thin-featured, wears a Colt in a flap holster on his left hip, army style?'

Alma nodded grimly. 'That's Toll Judkins, the man who's with Patch. Are you sure about all this?'

'Yeah, I'm sure. I was there. Is your husband about?'

'Cyrus? No. Why do you want to see *him*?'

'Courtesy.' Will gave a sarcastic grin. 'He might like to think about a pair of new top hands.'

'Why did they kill him, Will?' Alma asked.

'He was charged with treason by the cavalry. He stood trial, but was found innocent and freed. After the war, these scum came looking for someone to empty their poisonous bullets into. For too long, their sort didn't want the fighting to end . . . the killing to stop.'

Alma took a deep breath. 'I'm sorry, Will,' she said simply, and looked genuinely saddened. 'We really did fall out of love with each other. I know there's a lot of smart remarks you can make out of that, but we fought tooth and claw. I ran before we got serious . . . to gain another day.'

'So why did he stop loving you?'

'I don't think he ever started,' she said. 'He loved *you*, though, and because of it, wanted you to believe he loved me. But he didn't, and that's the truth, Will.'

As if distressed by the tension, the buckskin got fractious again, wanting to be on the move. Will was giving it some soothing words when an old man with a Yellowboy rifle stepped out from the side of the ranch house. He was wearing a pork-pie hat and a grubby cook's apron.

'This is a kid's piece, feller, but it'll drop you from here,' he rasped out. 'You all right, Mrs Oldring?'

'Get back in your corn crib, old-timer,' Will answered. 'Right now, I'm in not in the mood to have a gun pointed at me.'

'I'm fine, Wooly, go back inside,' Alma answered calmly. 'This young man is my son.'

Wooly allowed his jaw to drop. 'Honest? Your son? Wheew. Can't be right,' he said, 'talkin' that way to your ma an' all.'

'Yeah I know,' Will said. 'Now do as you're told. And put that rifle down,' he called out.

'You'd have got your horns clipped in my day,' the cook muttered, withdrawing truculently.

Alma settled a bemused expression on Will. 'Why don't you come in from the sun? I've got cool drinks inside,' she offered.

'There's one thing you can do for me, for Pa, for old times' sake,' Will said as an alternative to accepting.

'What's that, Will?'

'If I do happen to miss Patch and Judkins, and you see them before I do, don't tell them about me being here. It's hardly complicit. Maybe you owe us that.'

'If I do, you'll do something for me?' When Will said nothing, Alma continued. 'Before you leave Magdalena – as I know you will – allow me to tell you my side. Let me explain the life I had with your father. Maybe you'll better understand.'

For the shortest moment, a rebuff showed in Will's eyes, then it was gone. 'I'll think about it,' he said.

'You said there were *three* men.' Alma suddenly remembered Will's reason for wanting Oliver Patch. 'Who was the third?'

'The one I caught up with in Dixon Valedo,' he replied hoarsely. He turned his mare and cantered from the yard, heading for the western ridges.

Will cut across the grasslands, letting his mare have its head. By mid afternoon he was going down the far side of the ridges, his eyes quartering the range land ahead. He rode for another mile, then slowed to a walk, took a long pull from his canteen and let the mare chomp grass.

An hour later he was riding the Circle O's western boundaries, but, unknown to him, Oliver Patch and Toll Judkins were miles away, talking to a *pistolero* named Manuel Pinto.

Rufus Joad walked up to the front of Ambrose and Laurel Wale's home, and knocked.

When Laurel opened the door, he looked at her closely and grinned. 'This here town's just brimmin' with lovely ladies. They build some sort o' chute from Baltimore?'

Laurel frowned, and Joad realized he was being too familiar. 'I'm sorry, ma'am. I'm looking to see Sheriff Ambrose Wale,' he said, removing his hat.

'He's here, but not up and about,' Laurel replied. 'He's been unwell.'

'Yeah, I heard about it down at the saloon. I'll be but a short time, I promise. My name's Rufus Joad.'

Laurel looked hesitant. 'Yes, Will Sparrow's foreman. I know who you are.' She glanced past him, out at the gate as if expecting to see Will himself. 'You're welcome to come in, Mr Joad, but make sure there's no excitement.'

Joad nodded, stepping into the hallway. 'I was here in Magdalena about fifteen years ago,' he said.

'The time your father was elected sheriff. I'd just like to see him and pay my respects.'

'Oh. Did you know him well?'

'Not really.' Joad pulled at one of his ears. 'It's a long story, ma'am, but the gist of it is, your pa saved my life . . . not too far along from here, as I recall. In those days we'd call a street that ran through the town a *gunman's sidewalk*. Still, as I say, that was a long time ago.'

Laurel smiled. 'You're very like Will . . . generally,' she said tentatively.

Joad returned the smile. 'Ha, he'd probably say I was just like him. But in ten years, I'm sure he's picked up some of his own stuff. May I see your father now?'

'Of course.' Laurel opened the door to her father's room. 'Pa, there's someone here to see you. It's not a lady, but make yourself decent, anyway.'

Joad stepped into the room. He had an immediate look around, then his eyes met Wale's.

'Copperhead Joad,' the sheriff exclaimed after a moment's recall. 'Come in, come in. I always reckoned that law an' crime were natural bedfellows.' He gave a rumbling chuckle at his joke, then a grimace.

'He's Will Sparrow's ramrod, Pa,' Laurel said as Joad moved further into the room. 'He only got here today.'

'Sparrow's ramrod, eh?' Wale sounded incredulous. 'A famous McNelly Raider ramroddin' a bunch o' cow-an'-hay men.'

Joad gripped Wale's proffered hand. 'I've been that for ten years, Sheriff,' he confirmed. 'Like I've been plain *Rufus* Joad.'

'Yep, I hear you, an' I'm durn relieved.' Then a thought struck Wale. 'Will Sparrow's wearin' a gun rig with a C.J. brand,' he said.

'He bought it off me.'

'You teach him how to lift it as fast as you used to?'

'Well, you wouldn't live very long on the difference, that's for sure. Not that it's ever likely to come about.'

'I was hoping to see him tonight, Mr Joad,' Laurel said. 'Do you know where he is?'

Joad nodded. 'He told me he was riding out to the Circle O Ranch. I don't recall him saying a time he'd be back.'

'That's his mother's place. Did he say why he was going?'

'He's got some business with a man named Oliver Patch. Him and another feller,' Joad said quietly.

Wale frowned. 'We know all about that, Rufus; most of it, anyway. Did his father die the way he says he did?'

'Probably worse. You wouldn't want to go into detail over something like that.'

'Yeah, sure. I told him I wouldn't interfere, unless he shot 'em down in cold blood.'

'That's not likely. But in the circumstances, it's a principle where me and him are likely to differ.'

'Well, if he is coming, he should be here shortly.' Laurel didn't like the turn of the conversation, so she left the room. She lifted a shawl from the coat-stand inside the front door, walked out to the front gate to stand quietly in the cool of the night. After five minutes she shivered, found herself worrying about what Will had told her. Would he stay because of his feelings for her, or would he move on? *No, he'll come*, she thought, and smiled confidently through her chattering teeth.

16

An hour after dawn on Friday, Will rolled from the blankets in the corner of his hotel room and stretched. Hearing Rufus Joad's steady breathing coming from the bed, he turned his blankets into a neat bundle and piled them on the seat of the rocking chair. Then he poured water from the pitcher into a basin and noisily sluiced the upper parts of his body.

Joad stirred, opened sleepy eyes to look over at Will. 'You got in late last night,' he mumbled, licking his dry lips.

'I'd say it was early this morning.' Will spared him a quick glance as he buckled on his gunbelt. 'Besides, you're a ranch foreman, not a warden.'

Joad grunted, dropped his legs over the side of the bed, sitting for a moment watching his toes wriggle, before he pressed on. 'I didn't leave the sheriff's house until gone eleven,' he said. 'His daughter was outside waiting for something or somebody when I left. And it wasn't a night herder.'

Will stepped to the wall mirror, and ran a comb through his hair. 'Is that what you came all this way for, Rufus? To see what I'm up to in the . . . stakes?'

'Maybe. Are you and her getting serious, then?'

Will sat on the end of the bed and reached for his boots. 'How'd you like one of these for breakfast?' he said dryly.

'I'm only asking.'

'Well, don't. Let's go and get some food.'

'Yeah. Just give me a minute to put one or two things on.'

Ten minutes later they stood in front of the Beef 'n' Biscuit, and Joad read the notice tacked to the door. 'Closed. Elodie's Wedding Day'.

'Well, where do we eat now?' Joad asked. 'You know the town.'

'We could watch the world go by, wait to see if the saloon's got more than pickled eggs and corn dodgers.'

An hour later both men jumped to their feet when Cato opened the doors of the Rugosa.

'Morning, fellers. Mr Sparrow, what'll it be?' the barkeep asked as they eagerly fronted the bar.

'Two beers,' Joad told him. 'And clean glasses.'

'Don't do any other sort. Besides, it's a whisker early for dirty ones.'

'We come from Colorado,' Joad answered,

searching his pocket for coins.

While Cato poured their beers, Addison Rugosa came down the stairs and walked over to them.

'Good morning,' he said, addressing himself to Will. 'Looking for work?'

'No. Breakfast.'

'Fair enough. Take a table and I'll see what can be done.'

'That's a real accommodating feller,' Joad said from the corner table that Will often took. 'Why'd he think you were looking for work?'

'I must look that way, I guess. He says the same thing every time I come in here,' Will replied with a deceptive smile.

When they had finished their meal, Joad sat back and watched Will mop bacon fat from his plate. 'C'mon, tell me about Laurel Wale. Are you really paying attention to her?' he asked.

'As it means so much to you, yeah I am. It's that obvious, is it?'

'I noticed, didn't I? So, do you think you'll be coming back to the valley with a wife?'

'Yeah, maybe,' Will said as he stood up. With his fist, he banged good-naturedly at the crown of Joad's range hat, then went out to stand on the saloon's porch. He ground his jaw at the surge of impatience that now swelled in him. He wanted the job over and done with, and Rufus Joad's questions made it strongly affecting. His eyes raked the busying street as if phantoms of Oliver Patch and Toll Judkins were already looming towards him.

After a while, Joad came out and stood silently beside him.

'Yeah?' Will said, sensing that his foreman and friend had something to say that wasn't all cheery.

'Why don't you send me out to take care of 'em?' Rufus wanted to know. 'You could give me an order like a proper boss.'

'You've got to smarten yourself up for a wedding. If you make a good enough job of it, they might let you watch from a window somewhere.'

'Yeah, very funny. I should have known you'd come up with a smart-ass remark,' Joad retorted. 'Heh, you know I've never seen a live wedding. How about that?'

'Well, now's your chance, Rufus – see what real folk get up to,' Will said and stepped down into the street. 'Go back to the hotel. There's a bedside cupboard, and in one of the drawers you'll find a bottle of good whiskey. Make your acquaintance, and I'll see you later.'

Less than an hour later, west of Magdalena, Will topped a small rise, looking down and across a wide gully. He heeled his mare, sent it heading towards the land of the Circle O. He rode with little restraint, appreciating the open range away from the town and the ever-presence of its folk.

After another hour's ride, he reined in at the top of a long rise, dismounting in the shadowed cover of a cottonwood grove. He hunkered down, patiently waited until he saw Alma and Cyrus Oldring leave their ranch house and climb into the Dearborn. The couple were followed on by three riders, and Will guessed they were all headed for the marriage of Elodie Wesker and Cooter Lennon.

He stared until the carriage and riders were lost in the heat shimmer off the land. Then he waited for another quarter hour before mounting up and riding down to the yard.

Two men carrying rifles stepped from the bunkhouse door. Will sat unmoving in his saddle, waiting for them to say something or make the first move.

'Who are you, mister?' one of the men obliged. 'What do you want here?'

Will held up a hand in compliance. 'I'm looking for a couple of old partners.'

'Yeah? An' what makes you think they're out here?' the other man wanted to know.

Will nodded back in the direction from which he'd come. 'I heard in town. Whoa, girl,' he added as his mare shifted uneasily under him.

'Yeah? What did you hear?'

'That Oliver Patch and Toll Judkins are working at the Circle O. That's where I am, isn't it?'

The hands looked at each other, then back to

Will. 'They ain't here,' they said almost in unison.

'That's a shame. You see, I used to ride with 'em some years back,' Will lied.

The smaller, squat waddy gave Will a distrustful look. 'Yeah? You want 'em for somethin' particular?'

'No, just to chew some fat. Like I said, they're old trail buddies.' Will forced a smile. 'But if neither of them are here. . . .'

'That's right. Who shall we say was askin' for 'em?'

Will dragged up the face of the rebel corporal he'd killed in Dixon Valedo. 'Just tell them it was Lou,' he said. 'Lou Grissom.' He nodded once curtly, turned his horse from the yard and headed straight back to town.

Addison Rugosa walked out on to the porch of his saloon. He raised a foot to the deckchair, and lit a big cigar. With hard, slitted eyes, he watched the crowd gathering at the small church at the far end of the street. He saw Juno Hemsby go into the Wale home, emerging five minutes later with the sheriff, who was walking cautiously and had his arm in a collar-and-cuff sling.

Laurel followed them from the house, dressed neatly and carrying a small bunch of yellow paper-flower blossoms.

Rugosa guessed Cooter Lennon would already be up at the church, and ten minutes later he looked around to see the mercantile's rockaway carriage coming slowly down the main street. He nodded, smiled instinctively at the attractive figure of Elodie Wesker in her wedding gown, with her mother sitting beside her and Mose Baxter driving.

The saloon owner's expression hardened and he stepped down from the porch. He drew his stem-winder and noted the time, took another long look up and down the street, then walked slowly up to the church.

Twenty minutes later, three masked men pushed through the wide front door of the Magdalena Civic Bank. The two clerks snapped their heads up, gasped nervously at the drawn guns.

'That's it, keep the silence,' one robber advised them coolly.

Another man, taller and broader, stepped around the counter. 'On your feet, hands on your heads an' stay well back,' he commanded. Then he adeptly emptied the cash drawers, transferring the cash into two saddle-bags he had been carrying around his shoulders.

The third robber stayed quiet. He was keeping watch at the front window.

'Honcho man's out back hiding, is he?' asked the robber who had spoken first.

'No, he's at the wedding,' the scared teller told him. The youngster had a sheen across his pale face, and his hands trembled uncontrollably. 'One of us is the day's manager.'

'So one o' you's got the go-ahead to open the safe. Do it.'

The teller hesitated and, because of it, received a lash from the robber's gun barrel.

'Do as you're told. Open the goddamn safe.'

With the robber right behind him, the teller scrambled around his desk and over to the bank's, iron chest safe.

The second robber looked over at his colleague by the window. 'What's happenin' out there?' he called out in a loud whisper.

'Nothin' much. But hurry it up,' the lookout replied, turning around for a moment.

The other teller looked up when the man spoke. He saw the cloudy whiteness of the man's left eye, and immediately made a big mistake.

'Hey, I know you,' he blurted out. 'You're one of the line men from—'

Before he had time to say another word, Toll Judkins cursed. He jumped forward and swung viciously with the butt of his big Army Colt. The teller grunted, stumbled sideways against the counter, and Judkins hit out wildly again. The teller was caught across the temple as he fell; he was dying as he hit the floor.

Oliver Patch stepped back from the safe, tossing the saddle-bags over his shoulder. 'Get back behind the counter,' he barked at the other teller. 'Make one sound, an' I'll come back an' shoot you dead.'

The teller dropped the keys to the safe and moved away. He was panicky and his eyes were full of dread, a bruise already spreading from the ugly split across his cheek.

Quickly followed by Toll Judkins and Manuel Pinto, Oliver Patch hurried to the back door. He turned the lever, drew back the locking bar and opened it, peering into the lane before making a dash for the tethered horses.

The three men leapt into their saddles, riding further along the lane before turning back into the main street. From there they rode casually to Addison Rugosa's house, where Pinto dropped from his horse and caught the saddle-bags that Patch tossed him. The *pistolero* walked to Rugosa's yard, carefully stashed the bags in one of two wooden bins alongside the back stoop. He listened for a moment, gave a low satisfied grunt and returned to his horse. 'Work done. *Vamos*,' he said.

17

Will Sparrow closed the gate in the paling fence, and watched, waiting for the three horsemen to ride from sight. He'd been taking a quiet, less noticeable cut-through from the livery to the saloon, when he'd heard the hoofbeats approaching. Out of interest, he'd ducked out of sight, backed into someone's garbage area and watched with suspicious concern.

Now, he stepped into Rugosa's back yard and went straight to the box, the incident dawning when he saw the leather bags containing wads of stolen bank money. He stood up, threw the bags over his shoulder and, although it was in the opposite direction to which he'd been going, made his way to the side entrance of the jailhouse. He moved aside a stack of old bottle crates, pushed the saddle-bags in under the raised floor beams with the toe of his boot. 'Someone's looking down on me,' he muttered as he quickly moved the crates back.

When he walked calmly out on to the main street, he saw more or less what he expected to see. To the west, townsfolk were milling for the joyful occasion of the wedding; to the east, an angry crowd were gesticulating and yelling around the doors of the bank.

'The bank's been robbed, mister,' a man ran past, shouting. 'They've got away with thousands.'

Will sent a dry smile after him. 'Not very far, though,' he muttered.

The distraught, injured teller was telling Juno Hemsby what had happened, while Cooter Lennon was trying to calm the angry onlookers. Addison Rugosa was standing at the back of the gathering crowd, talking earnestly to one of the town's leading businessmen.

'I had more than five hundred dollars cash in that bank,' one man shouted.

'Yeah? Well I had a lot more'n that,' another voice contested.

Hemsby looked at the boisterous crowd, pulled his Colt Dragoon and fired a single shot in the air. 'Simmer down, all o' you,' he called out. 'We'll get your money back, an' the men who stole it. They couldn't have got far. For anyone that's interested, I'm raisin' a posse to ride in ten minutes.'

Laurel Wale was approaching the strident crowd when an arm slid around her shoulders and she was given a gentle hug.

'Have you lost much, Laurel?' Alma Oldring inquired of her.

'Not me, Mrs Oldring. But my father would have. I do hope they get it all back.'

Fifteen minutes later, twenty men, including Cyrus Oldring and Juno Hemsby, rode out of town.

Will didn't get involved with any of the excited, disorderly groups as he strolled towards to the saloon. He could have, could have told them that Juno Hemsby had it right, that they would recover the money and the men who'd stolen it. Whether they would be dead or alive was another thing, though. Presently, his information meant being a step ahead of both the sheriff's riders and the bank robbers, and that suited him just fine.

'You not riding with the posse then, Mr Sparrow?' barkeep Cato inquired with a cagey smile.

'It wasn't my money they took,' Will replied, more glibly than he'd meant. He paid for a beer and turned his back on the bar, leaning against it, watching the doors. A bunch of towners came in talking loudly and angrily. Rufus Joad was behind them. He saw Will and worked his way over.

'I bet you finished the whiskey,' Will said perceptively.

'Goddamn right, I did. Someone had already been at it, but half a bottle was better than none.' Joad scowled, taking Will's beer. He took a long pull, indicating another glass for Will. 'Is that all you got to say?' he added.

'Sorry. How about the wedding? Is Cooter Lennon a married man yet?'

Joad finished his beer in another gulp. He was going to take the other one that Cato handed Will, but thought better of it. 'The bank's been robbed and someone's made off with many, many thousands of dollars.'

'Yeah, but did Cooter and Elodie get to say "they did"?' Will said casually.

'Christ, Will, didn't you hear me? The bank's been robbed of most of the town's cash and whoever did it beat one of the tellers to death.'

'Yeah, Rufus, I know. Not about the teller – the robbery.'

'What the hell's going on here?' Joad demanded, waving for Cato to bring two fresh beers.

Will didn't reply. From the corner of his eye, he had seen Addison Rugosa enter the saloon and walk up the stairs to his personal and private rooms.

Moments later, Farley Rochester and a group of his ranch-hands came in, lined the bar and shouted for service. As Cato hurried down to them, Rochester sighted Will and ambled over.

'Good day, Sparrow. I was talking to the sheriff up at the church, and he tells me you're a ranch owner.'

'Yeah, I knew that.'

'Hmm,' Rochester uttered, unmoved by Will's

response. 'He said you've got land up in the San Louis Valley. That's a long way from here.'

'And here's a long way from there,' Joad interrupted.

Immediately, Rochester turned on the powerful man's stance when somebody interrupts, staring at Joad with silent, hostile scorn for a few long seconds.

Before Joad had time to make any response, Sheriff Wale came into the saloon. He wasn't wearing a Colt, but his free hand was gripped tight on his favourite revolver shotgun.

'Rochester. You had a lot o' money in that bank, just like the rest of us. Why the hell haven't you got any o' your men looking for them who ran off with it?' he snapped.

'I figured that was something for the law – your job, Sheriff.'

'It is, but you've got more'n a dozen men in your employ. I've but two deputies,' Wale retorted. 'I figured if you was to scour the hills to the west – land you know well – my boys could look elsewhere.'

The big rancher locked eyes with Wale for a moment, then nodded to the reasoning. He turned and went back to his men, spoke to them and they quickly finished their drinks. Rochester nodded once more at Wale, then Will, then followed his men from the saloon.

Wale turned his attention to Will. 'You two have good horses and guns; why not help?'

'Sorry, Sheriff,' Will replied. 'I was only just saying, that it's not my money or my town. And my pa always said to tend your own business first.'

'One day I'm going to meet someone who had a *dumb*-ass, instead of a *smart*-ass, pa,' Wale grated. He walked slowly from the saloon, spitting appropriate curses with each painful step.

Joad turned away from Will to watch the sheriff leave. 'Damned if that lawman ain't got a point,' he said. 'Say, Will, how did you know about the robbery?' he asked. But Will was walking towards the stairs, in the footsteps of Addison Rugosa.

'What the hell,' Joad muttered, giving Cato the nod. 'I guess you'll tell me when you're good and ready.'

Will walked quietly down the corridor and stopped at the door marked 'Private'. In one unbroken movement he turned the handle, opened the door and stepped into the saloon owner's office.

Rugosa was standing sideways on, looking down into the street from the window. 'What the hell are you doing up here?' he demanded.

'There's an important message I want delivered,' Will answered with an agreeable-looking smile.

'Message? You go find yourself a goddamn telegraph operator, feller, not one of my rooms that says *Private*.'

137

Will closed the door and moved towards the desk. 'This *is* private, and needs *your* personal touch, so sit down while I explain.'

Rugosa did as he was told, placing his hands in front of him on the desktop. 'What the hell do you want, Sparrow?' he levelled.

'Have you got yourself a cash-flow problem? Bar takings not doing so well?'

Rugosa looked up at Will, tapped his fingers. 'My saloon's doing just fine,' he retaliated. 'Just what the hell is it you want here?'

'Where's Manuel Pinto?'

'That's none of your business. Get to the point or get out,' Rugosa hissed, moving his hands off the desktop.

'Yeah, your time must be real precious. Earlier today I was wending my way through the alleyways, hoping to avoid all that to-do of the wedding, when I came upon three of your hired hands. They were running around excitedly with takings from the bank robbery.'

Rugosa became a sickly colour, and Will continued. 'One of them had the smart idea of stashing the loot in a box right outside of your very own back door, Mr Rugosa. Is *that* near enough to the point for you?'

The saloon owner now broke into a light, nervous sweat. 'There must be thirty thousand dollars in those saddle-bags, maybe more. I'm not a greedy man, Sparrow; deceitful and devious maybe, but not greedy. You can have ten per cent of whatever's there,' he offered with a lick of his dry lips.

Will shook his head. 'I don't wish for, or have any need of, that money,' he said quietly. 'It's Oliver Patch and Toll Judkins, I want.'

Rugosa's jaw dropped and his shoulders sagged a little with relief. 'I also know the value of my men. You're welcome to all *three*.'

'And *that*'s what I'd like you to tell them – the personal message I want delivered. Tell them if they want to see their ill-gotten dollars again, they have to have a meeting with *me*, Will Sparrow. I'll be downstairs waiting for them.'

'And do I get to collect the money if they decline the invitation?'

'They'll meet me. But if they *kill* me, no one gets rich.' Will crossed to the door. 'Remember, it's Patch and Judkins I'm interested in. As far as I'm concerned, Pinto can go his own way. It's up to him,' he said.

Rugosa was bewildered, but before he could ask any more questions, Will was gone, on his way back to the bar. A minute later, he was standing alongside Rufus Joad. 'Had to see a man about a couple o' dogs,' he said, with a cool smile.

18

It was nearly full dark that night when Alma Oldring left a friend's house in the town and walked along the main street. On the front porch outside of the Rugosa, Will Sparrow sat quietly on the bench. His legs were outstretched and his hat brim was pulled low across his face.

'That's how the pixies get you,' Alma said, stepping up on to the veranda.

'I would have seen them,' Will answered back. 'I was kind of hoping you'd walk on by.'

'Am I so intolerable, Will? There can't be many sons who would say that about their own mothers,' she said, leaning against the handrail.

'Only those with mothers like you.'

'At least you've accepted who I am. It's a start. You were going to visit us tonight. Have you had second thoughts about Patch and Judkins?'

'Not until hell freezes over. We're having a get-together, here tomorrow.'

'Oh.' She glanced up and down the street. 'The posse's not back yet.'

'I had noticed.'

'Do you really hate me, Will, or is it an act that for some perverse reason you've got to keep going?' she asked. 'Do you drop it all for Laurel Wale?'

'What the hell do you know about how I feel for Laurel? For anyone?'

'I know about the look on her face,' Alma said, trying not to sound affecting. 'She told me her father had his life savings in the bank . . . now it's all gone.'

Will tilted his head back and lifted the brim of his hat. For the shortest moment, Alma saw the concern in his clear grey eyes.

'That's bad luck. But the sheriff wasn't the only one to lose out.'

'He was the only one who set himself up to protect the town,' Alma said softly. 'I just thought you might have some concern. It looked like there was some for you, when *we* met . . . right here.' Alma tried a smile then. 'Ah well, there might be little sentiment, but at least you're not swearing and shouting tonight.'

'Yeah, I'm sorry about that. I guess the surprise must have worn off.'

'God, Will, I hope you didn't get that meanness from me. Is all this to do with Cyrus? He's a good man; he's good to me.'

'Yeah, well it's how good you are to him, that I'd be thinking about.'

'Everything your father did was for *you*, including the ranch. That was true enough, but I couldn't return anything to him. He had his son and that was all he wanted from me. Any feelings he had died when you were only five . . . when I left. Please don't believe everything he told you about me, Will. You must have learned there's always two sides. Cyrus showed me respect and kindness. Later that became love.'

Will listened, and a strange mix of doubts and maybes stirred inside him. 'I'm not about to throw my arms around you and say, "That's all right, then,"' he said, getting to his feet. 'You could have come back. To see me.'

Alma reached out, gripping Will's wrist. 'I tried to take you with me, but your father caught up with us before we'd reached the border. He put a bullet into Cyrus and took you back. He said that if he ever saw us again, he'd kill us both. That's why I never returned, Will. I didn't want to die. Not when I'd found another chance at my life.'

Will's face twisted with confusion. 'I don't know the right or wrong of it,' he said. 'All I know is that I've got a goddamn headache.' He stepped off the porch, walking into the darkness with a mix of thoughts and emotions swirling around inside his head.

Early the following morning, Cato had ridden out to one of the Circle O line cabins with the message that Addison Rugosa had given him. Just after first light, Oliver Patch read the words a second, then a third time. He crumpled the piece of paper in his hand and turned fierce eyes on the agitated barkeep.

'Damn him to hell,' he roared, snatching a fistful of Cato's shirt.

Cato squirmed in the tight grip. 'Yeah, I heard. I feel that way every time he comes into the bar. But don't take it out on me. I only brought the boss's message.'

Patch shoved the man roughly away from him and stepped to the open door. 'Goddamn you, Will Sparrow. Took you a while,' he seethed, his eyes quartering the open rangeland.

'So are you goin' to tell us what to do, Ollie?' From the low bunk he was resting on, Toll Judkins raised himself on to an elbow.

'We go in and see him like he wants. Only thing to do,' Manuel Pinto answered with a contemptuous laugh. 'But you better get him shot first. He won't give you a second chance.'

'How the hell do we get our money if we blast him?' Judkins glared nastily. 'You an' your stupid Mex ideas.'

143

Patch turned from the door. 'Button it, you two. Toll's right. We've got to turn the tables, 'cause it ain't a quarter share he's after. Cato, get some coffee started,' he added. 'You're not goin' anywhere just yet.'

Judkins swung his legs to the floor. 'How do we play it, then?'

'For the most part, the way Sparrow wants it,' Patch answered; then, turning to Pinto, 'He wants a face-off with me an' Toll. So are you throwin' in with us?'

Pinto nodded sharply. '*Si*. My argument's between him and the bag of money.'

'Then that just about settles it. We ride in before time.'

Judkins frowned. 'You been at the jimson, Ollie? He'll be layin' for us.'

'I know him,' Pinto said. 'Whatever happens, you won't get backshot.'

Patch turned to Cato. 'When do you open the saloon?' he demanded.

'Eleven o' clock's usual.'

'An' Sparrow's got a room at the hotel?'

'Yeah, Spanish Peaks.'

'Good. That's where we grab him – early.'

'Then what, Ollie?' Judkins asked.

'We go for a short ride, out o' town. Dancin' with a fat, barrel cactus should loosen his tongue.' Patch turned from Judkins to Cato. 'Hurry up with that

144

goddamn coffee,' he said. 'You'll be ridin' in with us. I don't want you shootin' off your barkeep's mouth.'

19

At first light, Will was standing in the hotel lobby with Rufus Joad. He was thinking about what Alma had told him about the sheriff's savings. Now he wanted Ambrose Wale to get his money back, something he hadn't fully considered earlier.

'It's a while yet before you meet your friends,' Rufus said, with the merest suggestion of doubt.

Will nodded. 'Yeah, some time after eleven,' he lied. 'Rufus, I told you last night I had the bank money but I wouldn't say where it was. Well, it's not far away. There's two saddle-bags stuffed under the jailhouse. Round the side, behind some boxes. Can you tell the sheriff?'

'Yeah, I'll tell him. Bearing in mind you're my friend as well as my boss, is there anything else I can do?'

'Not really. I was going to ask for a loan of your Colt, but you might be needing it.'

146

'What would *I* need it for?'

'If anything should happen to me, it'll probably be Manuel Pinto who does it. If it is, shoot him. In fact, shoot any of them left alive. And watch out for Rugosa. Like carrion, he'll wait for dead pickings before he makes a move.'

'I don't figure it, Will,' Joad said. 'They must know that if they shoot you dead, they don't get to find out where the money is.'

'Yeah, I know. That's what I started off hoping. It was my edge, one way of staying alive. But when they see me, that'll be the last thing on their minds. They all know that.'

Joad looked down at his tough, gnarled hands. 'Hmm. What if it all goes wrong and you do get to saddle a cloud?'

'Well, everyone's getting their money back for a start. And Wolf Run goes to you. There's a signed deed in this hotel's safe to confirm it.'

'I taught you everything I know about using a gun, Will. That gives you a chance. But there's three of 'em.'

'Patch and Judkins think they're on fighting wages, but they're not. That's my advantage, Rufus.'

For a long moment, Joad met Will's grey eyes, then without another word, he turned and left the lobby for the Wale house.

Will remained still for some time. He pulled his Colt and checked that everything was set and right,

147

wryly wondered how he'd mete out his six bullets. He tied down his holster, then walked unhurriedly out to the boardwalk, looking to the east, then west, away from the direction of the Rugosa Saloon. Not for one single moment had he intended to dicker with a trio of murderers and bank robbers. *If you're coming, make it soon, and the rising sun will just light up your faces*, he thought. Then he started his walk to the end of town, beyond the houses to the store barns and work sheds.

Nearly an hour later, Will saw Patch, Judkins and Pinto dismount and tie their horses at the water trough's hitchrail. He cursed silently, took a long deep breath, stepping closer in to the cover of a lean-to. The three men were together talking, and Will waited, easing his Colt in its holster. He counted to ten, then stepped out to where the main street broke into two northerly trails beyond town. He stood motionless, waiting for his heart rate to settle.

Manuel Pinto was the first to respond. '*Es el*,' he rasped. 'He was a step ahead, an' he's come to meet us. *Muy inteligente.*'

'Goddamnit, now we don't have a choice,' Patch murmured. 'We walk right on down the street, three abreast, brothers in arms.'

'*Cretino*, it's what he wants. You seen him with a gun?' Pinto sneered.

148

'I'm bankin' he's no better'n you. Move out. Don't walk slow and not too fast. I'll be a little behind in the middle. One of us is bound to nail him.'

'Which one of us is *he* goin' to nail?' Judkins complained.

'Shut it,' Patch snapped. 'Pinto, take the left. You call it, an' go for your guns at the same time. That'll give him a decision to make. If you don't bring him down, I will.'

From fifty paces away, Will started his walk. As the distance between them closed, he drew his Colt, flicking his eyes backwards and forwards between the three men. As they came on, Pinto and Judkins fanned away from Patch, stopping when they were less than thirty feet from Will.

Will estimated that Manuel Pinto would be the one to shoot first. But the Mexican was smart, standing out to Will's right. Will would be twisting awkwardly to get off a good shot, and that's when Judkins would try for him. Patch would take a fraction longer, make the opportunist killing. *Time to find out*, he thought, as the realization dawned that Pinto was letting Judkins make the first move.

When Judkins dropped his hand to make a draw, Pinto corresponded with his own Colt.

Knowing that he couldn't do much about Pinto's first shot, Will brought up his Colt. His first bullet struck Judkins low in the neck. The impact sent the man back, dropping to the ground with his gun unfired.

Pinto's gun roared, chewing flesh from Will's left shoulder. But Will was into a sidestep and sending a shot back. Pinto dived, but Will's bullet had already ploughed deep into the middle of his chest. The Mexican rolled once, attempted to raise himself, his gun hand twitching helplessly until his final, lifeless collapse.

The air buzzed, as Oliver Patch fired two hurried shots. *Christ, I thought you'd have run,* Will thought as one bullet ripped through his shirt, bruising the flesh around his waist. He took a breath, watched tensely as Patch ran towards a gap between two wagon repair shops.

Blood was now running from Will's left shoulder, across and down the front of his shirt. 'Another set o' ruined duds,' he gasped. He made a diagonal run for one side of the shadowy gap, stood with his back pressed hard against the upright of a lean-to.

A few seconds later, Patch's voice called out. 'If you want me, Sparrow, you'll have to come an' get me.'

Will figured him to be hiding somewhere among the spare wheels, braces and wagon boards. 'Lose your nerve at the last minute, Patch? Happens when you're up against someone who's got a gun in their hand,' he taunted.

There was no answer, and Will grimaced as pain beat through his shoulder and side. He edged further back into the lean-to, saw a door leading to the adjoining workshop. He turned the handle, pushed quietly against the door and stepped inside. He waited until his eyes grew accustomed to the gloom, then moved silently to the rear entrance.

The back door led into a yard stacked high with green lumber, most of it creating a boundary marker alongside the wagon repair shop. He listened, heard nothing, then stepped up on to the boards for a look over the top.

Patch was sideways on, crouching behind a big, broken wagon wheel.

Will pushed his Colt into his holster, placed both hands on the top of the timber pile and swung up and over. He landed on both feet, drawing his gun at the same time.

Patch whirled, shooting fearfully, with no composure or accuracy, and his bullets thudded into the stacked timber.

Will's first shot sank into Patch's side, his second beneath his outstretched arm. Patch's knees buckled and he tried to bring up his gun for a final shot, but he was finished, rolling forward into the hard-packed dirt.

As Will stepped over to him, the dying man turned his head, eyes opening and closing. 'Never was the money, was it, Sparrow,' he said throatily. 'I should've known.'

'Yeah, you should,' Will rasped back. 'You're dead because you murdered my pa, nothing else. I just hope he's somewhere watching, you son-of-a-bitch.'

With his near-empty Colt hanging at his side, Will walked from the workshop. He looked thoughtfully at the body of Manuel Pinto, turning the *pistolero* over with the toe of his boot. 'Thanks for bringing them to me,' he said, looking down at something like a resigned smirk across the dead man's lips. 'You should have found some other employ, you and your brother.'

He walked over to Toll Judkins. The man with the moon-eye was staring sightlessly up at the sky, blood already congealing from the messy hole in his neck. 'And what did it get *you*? Even lice die in the end,' he muttered cynically, pushing his Colt back into its holster.

20

Will looked back towards the town and saw his mother making her way along the boardwalk, her step anxious and faltering. Laurel was on the other side of the street, standing beside her father and Rufus Joad. A few onlookers were staring, both anxious and nonplussed, towards the gunfire.

It was a movement from the balcony fronting the upper floor of the Rugosa Saloon that caught Joad's watchful notice.

'I'd be grateful for a loan of that ol' cannon you're so fond of toting around,' Joad suggested to Wale. 'I think I've sighted an ill-intention.'

He checked there was a cartridge in the firing chamber of the big revolver shotgun, cocked the hammer and lifted the barrel. The seconds ticked by as he waited, then with careful aim, he fired.

Addison Rugosa made no sound as he was hit, blasted from the front to the side of his office balcony. Still clutching his rifle, he crashed through the painted railings, falling in a bloodied, lifeless heap to the street outside his saloon.

From nearly fifty yards away, Will cursed, moved his hand quickly back to the butt of his Colt. He took in the scene, then started towards the group of townsfolk who were slowly approaching from the edge of town.

Laurel was running to meet him. 'Where's all the blood come from?' she gasped, startled at the sight of Will's torn, bloodstained shirt. 'Are you hit?'

'Walking wounded, nothing more. *This* is for those inquisitive chinwaggers,' he said, slipping an arm around her shoulder.

'You OK, Will?' Joad asked him. 'You never were one for a tidy appearance.'

'Yeah, I'm fine, Rufus. And thanks.'

'I knew there'd be something I could do, and you told me to watch Rugosa. I just put the two together.'

'Any need for me to go take a look?' Wale asked.

'No. You can send a gravedigger if you like.'

Wale's eyes narrowed. 'You kill 'em fair like I told you?'

Will held the man's demanding stare. 'I'm not sure about fair; there was only three of them. I told you, you'd be one of the first to know when my business was done, Sheriff. Well, now it is.'

Wale made a grim smile and nodded. 'OK. I'm

not about to thank you for litterin' up the town with bodies. But I will for gettin' its money back – sincerely.'

'It never was anyone else's, Sheriff.'

'He's dead, so off the record, why the hell would Addison Rugosa ever be a part in all this?' Wale pondered.

'I guess he was one of those who thought you could never have too much. He told me that life here wasn't like Sunday School. Well, he was right about that. Lucky for me, Rufus was only doing as he was told.' Will let go of Laurel and with his right hand ushered her towards her father. 'If you have the choice, try and tell your daughter why it's best to stay out of harm's way,' he said. Then he turned and headed for the livery.

Joad handed the shotgun back to Wale, then went after Will. 'You should let the doc take a look at those flesh wounds,' he advised, on catching him up.

'He can look at anything he wants if you get him to the livery before I'm saddled,' Will answered back.

Ten minutes later, in the light of the open doors, and under the constraints of protest and impatience, Doc Cotton tended to Will's injuries best he could, with what he carried in his bag. When he'd finished, Will paid him, and went straight to his buckskin mare.

'Thanks, Doc,' Joad said on Will's behalf. Then, turning to Will, asked, 'What are you going to do now? Where are you going?'

'Home. It's what I said I'd do.'

'Yeah, but things have changed. You can't just ride off like that.'

'Why not?' Will threw his saddle blanket over the horse's back.

'There's others to think about. Young Laurel for one. Alma – your mother.'

Will took the saddle down from the stall railing, paused thoughtfully for a moment, then tossed it up and over on to the mare's back. 'You said you wanted a hands-on boss again. Well, after two years, you've got one. Make up your mind.'

'It seems to me that recently, you might have said a few things you didn't rightly mean,' Joad countered. 'Goddamnit, Will, you're turning your back on good people. Surely you owe them a few minutes to explain. I'd certainly like to hear why you're leaving them.'

Will pulled determinedly on the cinch. 'Stick to what you're good at, Rufus. I don't owe anybody anything,' he said. 'Now, are you going to saddle up, or stay here and play the go-between?'

Joad opened his mouth to continue his argument, but Laurel entered the livery and he let it go.

'Will?' she said with obvious surprise. 'Are you leaving?'

'I'm going away, yes,' he answered without looking around.

'You got me to talk with Pa so you could ride off? Am I going to see you again?'

'I don't know. I can't answer that.'

'You didn't mean those things you said?'

Will looked at her, saw the cheerless face, the glistening eyes. 'Yeah, I meant them. But I also said you wouldn't like to live on an uncertainty. The uncertainty was *me*, Laurel. I've just killed three men. Is that the sort of man you want to settle down with?'

'I know why you did what you did. I don't blame you for it. A court would have used a rope, but it would have been the same end.'

'Does that mean your father will let me ask for your hand?'

'Yes. If it's what I want, he'll allow it,' she said, looking for something in Will's grey eyes.

'Glad to know I figure in some things happenin' round here,' Wale voiced as he walked into the livery.

Will coughed, took his eyes away from Laurel. 'Sheriff, I want your daughter for my wife . . . I want that very much.'

Wale nodded. 'I guess you get most things you set your mind to, young feller. Would be there anythin' else for me to get used to?'

'A couple of things,' Will said. 'Get rid of that badge and big old shotgun. Any father-in-law of

157

mine won't be needing them where we're headed. Leave the town to Juno Hemsby.'

Wale stared hard at the ground around his feet for a moment. 'I'll swear him in the moment he gets back. First deputy can go to young Cooter – a weddin' present from me. I'll need a wagon or two.'

Leading his mare, Will and Laurel walked out into the bright sunlight. They saw Alma Oldring standing in front of the Spanish Peaks Hotel.

'Take my horse, Laurel. Tie him to your front fence. I'll see you soon,' Will said, and handed over the reins.

He returned Alma's smile as he approached the hotel. 'I guess you did right by leaving with Oldring. I'm sorry for the way I spoke to you.'

'Thank you, Will. I wasn't about to start telling lies after so many years. Truth has a way of coming out in the end.'

'You and your husband . . . Cyrus, should come and visit Wolf Run sometime. You know the way.'

'Yes, it's not the sort of trail I'd forget. Goodbye, Will, and good luck.'

Will walked from his house to the middle of Wolf Run's big yard. He looked all around him, then back to the three men who were sitting the corral fence.

'Jake, ride out to the western pastures and drive those Herefords up to the tanks. Take three men with you,' he shouted.

'Yes boss.'

'Dutch. You'll be going into town to get the provisions. And don't come back saying you got waylaid by some whiskey drummer.'

'Yes, boss.'

'Rufus. Can you get a crew together and start on the new barn? First winter snow's not so far off, and we'll need the feed storage.'

'Yes, boss.'

Up on the veranda, Ambrose Wale rocked back in his chair, and chuckled.

Will heard him. He turned with a slow smile, then looked towards his wife, who was standing in the doorway.

Laurel crooked a finger. 'And you, Will Sparrow, get yourself up here to check these tally sheets.'

Will grinned. 'Yeah, I will. You just make sure there's a big open can of sliced peaches waiting for me.'

'Yes, boss; whatever you say, boss,' she said, sharing the cheerful moment with her pa.